Lock Down Protocol

J.T. Fluhart

First paperback edition July 2023

ISBN 978-1-7364741-4-3(paperback)
ISBN 978-1-7364741-6-7 (hardback)
ISBN 978-1-7364741-5-0 (eBook)

For Tiff and all those who support me.

Chapter One

New York City
10:00 PM

Cleo, at least that's what the two legger called her before she tossed her out into this nasty, cold alleyway, continued rummaging through the steel dumpster for her dinner. These large containers had replaced her dainty little plastic bowl as her food source. There was a time not long ago when she was waited on hand and foot.

Twice a day her favorite two legger with long dark hair would call to her, "Here, kitty, kitty! Come get your breakfast!" or, "Come, Cleo, let's get your dinner! Yum, yum!"

Most times Cleo would be stretched out in a warm patch of sunlight on a windowsill. She'd make an easy drop to the floor, then an exaggerated stretch giving her best Halloween pose that arched her back before darting toward where her name was being called. As she would round the corner into the kitchen to her dainty food bowl, her favorite two legger would shake that eye-catching emerald-and-ruby-colored bag over her dish, releasing the flow of those yummy little morsels of her favorite chicken-flavored food. The two legger would stroke her back and tail as Cleo dove into her twice-a-day feast. Later she would curl up in the two legger's lap for more attention as she would purr contently with her belly full.

One day that all changed. Two leggers were everywhere moving all the contents of her home out into a large rumbler. Those rumblers terrified Cleo as they raced around her with their sudden bursts of angry beeps and ear-piercing screeches when they stopped. Her favorite two legger gave her hugs and kisses, then tearfully let her down on the cold, dirty concrete of this alleyway. She turned and left Cleo there frightened. Cleo's senses were overloaded with her new surroundings. She raced for the shelter of a fire escape platform. She stayed under there for three days, too terrified to move until hunger drove her out. When would her favorite two legger come back? What had Cleo done so wrong to be shunned into this filthy, loud, lonely place? Nothing. Not a damn thing. She was loyal and loving. She had given that wretched two legger all her affection, especially when the wetness streaked down her face, which was so often it seemed. Cleo would run to her and lick the salty liquid with her coarse tongue. The two legger would smile and sniff, then laugh and cuddle Cleo close as she showered her furry friend in gratitude. Cleo was always there. Always loyal.

She continued digging around in the dumpster. Her stomach rumbled as she picked up the scent of something spoiled in a paper bag. She used her claws to tear it open. Inside was about a two-legger bite of a hamburger. To Cleo this was a real feast. She devoured it quickly before the smell found its way to her competition—the huge subway rats. Individually they were weak, but in packs they were vicious. If they saw her hunched over anything edible, they would attack her. Their beady little eyes were everywhere. Even now she could feel them watching her, letting her expend her precious energy to find the food so they could come overtake her and steal it, leaving her tired and starving.

But tonight things were in her favor as she finished the small feast uninterrupted. However, she felt she may regret it. The food was slimy and tasted a bit sour. Sometimes what food she found she regretted eating, but it was either a moment of nausea or the hard pangs of starvation. Nine times out of ten she chose nausea. But maybe she should have passed on this find because her body began to tingle all over. Inside her chest it began to burn, which spread throughout her limbs, overtaking the tingling. She felt faint and thought she might suffocate as she gasped for air. Everything went from one extreme to the other inside her body. She went from near suffocation to breathing more deeply than ever. This increased flow of oxygen made her feel strong and more alert. Her shaky legs grew firm, and she stood tall in the dumpster. She reached up with her front paws with ease, vaulted over the dumpster's edge, and gracefully landed on the gritty concrete. She stood still, taking in her surroundings with heightened abilities. What had happened to her? Sounds of scraping on the alley wall across from her peaked her now very sensitive hearing.

What is that noise? Cleo thought to herself. Her lean lips curled back in irritation, revealing long double fangs that slightly curled back to a needle's point.

She jerked her head toward the scraping noise and focused on a small beetle scurrying across the bricks. Its little claws tap-danced across the mortar. She found she could see in beautiful clarity. The beetle's hard shell shimmered yellow, green, and purple as the light of the brilliantly white moon shined on it. She looked up at the huge, bright moon overhead and let its glow wash over her. She purred a deep baritone sound that reverberated in the alleyway as she relished the powerful sensation it gave her.

To her left she picked up the faintest whiff of the rank odor that always sent her running. This smell meant danger. It meant whatever food she had found she better gulp down quickly and move on. This smell was the smell of the huge subway rats she feared to her core. And by the stench wafting over her now, she knew there were several bogies inbound. But for some reason, tonight she wanted the fight. She desired the confrontation.

"Bring it on, rat bitches," she hissed. She stood on her strong legs and waited. Her long, thick tail slowly moved from left to right, playfully.

The pack of rats confidently rounded the far corner. More and more came around. The lead rats stopped hard, causing the group behind them to topple over themselves. They all froze as their beady eyes locked with Cleo's in confusion. She hissed violently. Her lips snarled wide, showing off row after row of razor-sharp teeth. They pissed themselves in fear and scattered in all directions like a dish shattering on the ground.

Disappointed, Cleo contemplated giving chase. She wanted to run and feel her lean, strong body release the tension coiling up inside her body. Just as she was about to take off after the rats, her sensitive hearing picked up another sound behind her, a sound that caused her body to react in hunger. Her enhanced killer instinct took control of her brain, putting her on autopilot. These noises aroused something inside her she couldn't control. Her body flushed and adrenaline poured into her bloodstream, causing her heart to thump harder in her chest. All of her senses heightened off the charts. She silently crept into the shadows behind the dumpster, sat, and waited patiently for her prey.

"Would you please stop it, Dan?" the blonde woman said as she shooed the man's hand off her ass for the third time since they left the bar three blocks ago.

"What? Come on. You know you've been wanting the chance for us to hook up." The man pulled her into the alley's shadows.

"This was just supposed to be Friday night drinks. Not a hookup," she said, flustered.

"What was that kiss in the office the other day? Huh, tell me?" The alcohol on his breath was strong.

"I don't know. Really I don't," she said as Dan backed her against the brick wall. He pressed himself against her and leaned in for a kiss. She relented as their lips touched, then timidly kissed back.

Maybe not so bad after all, she began to think. She committed her mouth further. Dan moved his right hand up her body and gently squeezed her ample left breast. He moaned into her kiss and squeezed it harder.

"I don't know about this," she said, breaking the lip lock and looking around. "We are in an alley, for goodness sake."

"Just do me a favor. No one is around," Dan said without even looking to check. "Come on, please," he urged again. He took her wrist and moved it behind his belt, into his pants.

Her fingers felt his excitement as he pressed it against her palm.

"That's it. Just give it a rub."

"Ok, we're done here. I'm not doing this in an alley." The blonde lady tried to pull away, but Dan held her hand against his crotch.

"Won't take but a second. Squeeze it," he urged.

"Stop it, Dan. You're drunk and will regret this behavior next week," she tried to reason with him, but the brain in her hand was in full control of him now. He pressed her hard against the bricks.

"Squeeze it!" he demanded. "Do it for me, please."

Her head hit hard against the wall and she yelped in pain. This had gone too far. "OK, Dan, easy," she breathed. He felt her fingers begin to cooperate as pleasure shot up his core. He released her wrist, and thankfully her fingers stayed wrapped in place.

"Oh yes," he moaned. He leaned back in for those soft lips again.

If he wanted her to squeeze something, then she would. But it wouldn't be the frank. She would squeeze the beans. With that thought she cupped her hand lower and felt his grapes, swollen with excitement and ready to burst. She found the left one and then squeezed with all the strength she had.

"Aww, shit! SHIT!" he screamed in shock and doubled over, dropping to his knees. He was trying to talk, but nothing came out but painful groans.

"Sorry, but you made me do that. Now go home and sleep this off." She turned and walked away. Over her shoulder she said back to him, "Sober up and I'll forget this ever happened. I'll see you on Monday." Then she was gone. Dan lay on the filthy asphalt coughing in pain.

From behind the dumpster Cleo watched the event unfold. Her senses could smell the scent of the woman the man seemed to be crazy for. It was revolting and overpowering to Cleo. It reminded her of her favorite dark-haired two legger. She, too, covered herself in such an offensive smell each morning. The man exuded another smell entirely, but she had to search for it through the cloud of booze in the air around him. As Cleo's keen nose waded in deeper, she detected something more primal. It was a musky animalistic aroma, and that excited her, especially at the moment he screamed out. The smell intensified, and she licked her chops in anticipation. Her hunting instinct held her in place. *Patience*, it told her. Her chance to roll in his primal delight would come soon enough.

9

The blonde-haired two legger walked away, leaving the yummy one writing around on the ground. Cleo positioned her feet underneath her and waited for the perfect moment to pounce. Dan finally raised to all fours and coughed, fighting back his puke. He could still feel the blonde woman's thumb and forefinger pinch the fire out of his left testicle. He lowered himself down again as if worshiping the alleyway as another wave of nausea enveloped him. He sobbed in pain. He feared she may have torn his precious jewel loose.

Cleo silently stalked forward. She could smell the same salty liquid her favorite two legger used to leak from her eyes. This one leaked it from his eyes too. For a split second she wanted to rush over and cuddle him and use her prickly tongue to lick his face and make it all better. But her lizard brain fought against the urge.

Nah, I need to eat. She let out a low feral growl.

In the alleyway her growl echoed deep. Dan felt it as much as heard it. He looked up slowly. The sound reminded him of visiting the tiger cage at the zoo as a kid. Their growls were rooted in pure strength. As he looked at the animal before him, the pain of his smashed testicle lost its priority. What he saw before him invoked a more powerful grip on his body, one of utter and complete terror. He sat up slowly. Grit and pea gravel stuck to his outstretched palms as he held them out toward the beast.

"OK, fella. Take it easy now," Dan coaxed. Before him was a cat. That much he could tell, but barely. Its eyes were very large and glowed with a deep golden color like it was staring into a spotlight. Its whiskers were long as they bounced in tandem with the lips sneering hard on its thick muzzle. The teeth had his full attention. This creature's mouth was full of them. Row after row, razor sharp and serrated to a needle's point. He slowly stood and backpedaled out of the alleyway. What crushed testicle? Dan's testicle was fine. Better than ever.

The abomination of a cat shrieked a scream so viciously loud Dan could feel his sprinting heart rattle in his chest. Then quick as lightning, it leaped on him.

Cleo couldn't resist the need to scream her excitement and have some fun. She leaped at least a dozen feet into the two legger's face. She pushed out her elongated claws into the sides of his head, and they easily pressed through his skull. The immediate resistance of the bone quickly gave way to warm softness inside. Cleo pressed them deeper until her paws and his head were fused together.

Dan could feel one of the needle-like claws enter through his cheek. The more he screamed, the more the claw sliced his tongue until it severed and flopped out of his mouth. He fell onto his back, kicking and punching the beast. Finally, he grabbed its skin under its dense fur and tugged with all his strength. Cleo moved her spine up and down, enjoying the back scratch. Her hind claws gripped the two legger's rib cage like her old scratching post. It felt great feeling her long claws extending out fully. A low purr vibrated out of her chest. Yes, she needed this. Just as she thought she might adjust her grip to play with the two legger a bit longer, he grabbed her tail and gave it a vicious yank. Cleo screamed and opened her jaws wide and crunched into Dan's face, removing a huge chunk of it.

Dan's reaction was to twist and yank Cleo's tail like his life depended on it, because it did. Cleo retracted the claws on her left paw, releasing it from Dan's head, then pushed them out again to their fullest, deadliest length. With speed not of this world, she shredded Dan's neck until his head disconnected from his body, still stuck to her right paw. Panicked, she shook her paw like it was on fire and hopped around until the head freed itself and bounced off the brick wall. She stood there breathing heavily, gaining her composure. Blood quickly pooled around her. Its coppery smell made her stomach twist in hunger. She lowered her head and began lapping it up eagerly like she loved to do with the occasional saucer of creamy milk her favorite two legger sometimes rewarded her with. After several minutes to get her fill, she sat up and began cleaning the blood off her paws with her long, prickly tongue. She missed this feeling of fullness, contentment. She stood and gave an arched Halloween pose that stretched her back and legs, thinking, *That was fun.*

Moments later her heightened hearing picked up the voices of more two leggers out in the darkness.

Oh hell yeah. I can do this all night, Cleo thought as she stalked after the voices.

Chapter Two

Reynosa, Mexico

The sun wouldn't rise for another few hours. Mel
yawned into her hand. She was sitting at a large
rectangular conference table in a room atop an airport
control tower. The tower was built into the corner of the
compound they were in called La Casa Ballerinas and
oversaw air traffic on its small runway strip. From here
they could see for miles in all directions, as the room had
thick glass walls on all four sides. On one side of the
room, surrounded by glass, was the elevator that served as
the only entrance.

In the distance, hung low in the sky, was a huge,
brilliantly white shining moon. Even at this wee morning
hour, it looked like early afternoon outside. Here and
there gunshots popped in the distance, sometimes in
rapid succession. Next to Mel, her brother Rob sat
slumped in a high-back chair with his head back. His

mouth gaped open like a Venus flytrap. A slight snore emanated from his nose. Mel wished she could sleep. She was exhausted, but the events leading up to her arrival at La Casa Ballerinas had her wired. In the center of the table was a conference phone spread out like an octopus. Several voices could be heard from it, conversing quickly in Spanish. Around the phone were large maps of the surrounding counties, and men dressed in navy blue fatigues were bent over them, marking and writing notes as they listened to the voices from the phone.

The elevator dinged announcing the arrival of a guest. Rob jerked awake and blinked his eyes into focus. He wiped the drool from the corner of his mouth as the elevator doors opened and revealed an old woman in a wheelchair. Her lap was covered in a faded blanket that Rob knew was once brilliantly colored. She was pushed into the room by a younger lady dressed scrubs like a nurse. Everyone immediately quieted and stood. One man pushed a button and silenced the noisy phone. No one spoke as the nurse-looking lady wheeled the old woman to the head of the table. Missing her ring finger, she rested the other nine on the table's smooth top. They look twisted and frail from the toll arthritis had taken on them.

Erma Florchett, now pushing one hundred years old, took in the scene around the table. Her eyes were alert as she moved them from one face to another, settling them on Rob and Mel, her reunited grandchildren. A smile slowly creased her wrinkled face, then faded as she turned to the leader in the room. He was a large, gray-haired man wearing paramilitary fatigues with captain's bars on his lapels. For the benefit of her grandchildren she spoke in English.

"Please sit," she said mildly to everyone. Once the sounds of murmurs, chairs scooting, and papers being rustled subsided, she turned to the captain and said, "My dear cousin, please bring me up to speed since initiating the Lockdown Protocol," she said in a voice that was soft but commanding.

The Lockdown Protocol was a series of offensive and defensive measures planned out nearly fifty years ago by a small well-trained and well-equipped law enforcement team called the Rurales. They were headquartered here in the La Casa Ballerinas compound outside of Reynosa, Mexico. Every year since the protocol's creation, it was practiced and updated to keep pace with advancements in technology and weaponry. Tonight the Rurales top brass gathered around this conference table in semi-disbelief its purpose had manifested itself. However, they were nonetheless still focused on its execution. All officers present were from subsequent generations of the Lockdown Protocol's founders. Many had not fully believed its reason for existing until witnessing the events of this night. As kids, the stories of El Gallo de Satanás, or Satan's Rooster, seemed too much like a Brothers Grimm fairy tale to be true. They assumed it was only told to scare children into performing their farm chores. But what was currently transpiring outside the compound's walls was real. Now each of them was glad the protocol was created and maintained, or death would most likely be upon them and their families within these four walls. The Rurales' best data analysts discussed sitreps, or situational reports, on the conference phone that confirmed this reality all over the country. Two large flat-screen TVs hung opposite the elevator were split into multiple squares. Each showed newscasts of the carnage this night brought all around the world. This was no fairy tale.

Taking Erma's cue to speak in English, the captain cleared his throat and began his report to her. "We have confirmations of animal mutations from all over Mexico. Our contacts abroad have confirmed them as well, now that the entire globe has reached 10:00 PM or surpassed it." He clasped his hands together and continued, "As the supermoon recedes back into its original orbit, we are not seeing any animals reverting back to normal as hoped." He paused to let the grim information sink in before he continued.

Erma's eyes remained locked on her cousin as everyone else's seemed locked on her. What she had endured that night fifty years ago on a tiny scale was unimaginable. Rob and Mel were astonished at how she kept her composure hearing these gruesome details of that hideous night being churned up on a global scale now. An animal apocalypse.

"We've lost two men so far and another five injured," explained the captain. Just as he continued speaking, a huge BANG! slammed into one of the glass windows. It shook the entire room. There were shouts of surprise. The nurse-looking lady shrieked loudly. Rob instinctively ducked, then turned to see what had happened behind him. There was another BANG! The window cracked in all directions.

"What is that thing!" someone shouted as folks began to scramble away from the window. An ear-piercing screech filled the room as huge chunks of glass the size of baseballs exploded in all directions. Two people were struck by the sharp shards, sending them bloodied to the floor. Fortunately, the high backs of Rob's and Mel's chairs blocked the deadly objects from hitting them. Mel pulled a stunned Rob under the table for cover from the chaos. Through the window a huge winged beast grabbed an officer in a massive talon and crushed his skull, sending brain matter in all directions. It had a huge serrated beak and used it to slash another officer across his chest, nearly cutting him in half.

Up until a few days ago, Rob suffered from a repetitive nightmare that robbed him from any meaningful sleep, that nearly sent him insane. Under the table he was stricken with fear as he watched this bloody scene unfold. He was completely terrified in recognition of this beast . . . It was the rooster abomination from that nightmare here and now. It had white-and-black feathers with a huge bright red comb atop its head that was razor sharp. Each of its massive claws consisted of six huge fishhook-shaped toes and was slicing through anyone within reach of them. Eyes wide, Rob was paralyzed.

****

Jose Martinez stood on the first floor guarding the entrance to the elevator bank. Given the highest-ranking officers in the Rurales were gathered upstairs in the conference room *and* the Lockdown Protocol was in effect, security was at its highest level. His assignment was to stand guard, verifying visitors and reporting anything strange, anything out of the ordinary. He was two hours into his watch and determined to keep alert, but his mind drifted back to when he signed up with the Rurales. Then, he was with a small police outpost outside Mexico City. The Rurales were legendary in their fight against cartel corruption. They were the gold standard in law enforcement within Mexico. As a kid his dream was to join the Rurales and fight corruption for his country. Since joining the Mexico City police, he was sick of seeing his fellow officers succumb to the bribes and decadence of the cartels. Jose had applied at least a dozen times to

20

take the Rurales entrance exam. He was shocked when he was finally accepted. He knew it wasn't a guarantee he would make the elite group, but only a rare opportunity to take the exam. He was determined to give it his all and pass.

The exam consisted of more than physical capabilities. He was tested on his knowledge of Mexican law and police procedures. They gave him extensive psych tests that pushed his mental endurance. But what he found the most interesting was the testing of his country's founding and history. They measured his convictions for Mexican patriotism. It was said the Rurales were immune to corruption, which explained why the majority of the entrance exam was focused on this topic. This was the hardest part of all to pass because it was deceptive and tricky because he had grown up in stark poverty. Mexico has the highest poverty rate in North America. Its economy is based on commodities and manufacturing, and it has the second-highest degree of economic disparity between the wealthy and the poor. So one might think it easy to resist cartel corruption because it is the right thing to do, but what starts as a slippery slope quickly ends up in a landslide.

Jose remembered with clarity the letter he'd received that said he had passed his exams and was accepted into the Rurales probationary program. That program lasted for one year then he would receive full authority. During this first year he pulled what could be considered grunt duty, the most boring and mundane assignments. But he didn't care; he was a part of the most elite law enforcement team in Mexico. One thing he quickly appreciated was the high-tech weaponry the Rurales had access to. Being closely aligned with the United States Drug Enforcement Agency, their standard-issue weapons were far more advanced than the Mexico City police's. His standard-issue rifle was the same as the United States Special Forces', an M4A1 AR-15. He had never shot such a weapon with such precision in his whole life. He loved his gun and quickly became very accurate and practiced in its use. This honed skill would be needed more in the next few minutes than any other day in his career. Being assigned guard duty of the control tower elevator bank, he knew it was a boring assignment. He took such boring assignments seriously. He was eager to advance in the ranks.

His radio crackled to life. It was his captain screaming to come up to the conference room, as the occupants were under attack. He jerked from his thoughts and wondered how they could be in danger up there? No one went up the elevator since Senorita Erma just a few minutes ago. The terror coming through his earpiece compelled him to get moving. He entered the elevator and punched the conference room floor on the panel. Nervous sweat trickled down his back as the elevator took its sweet time riding up a dozen floors. Finally, it dinged signaling the conference room level. The doors opened, revealing the bloodiest scene he had ever seen. The aggressor was a beast like nothing he ever imagined could exist in this world. The death it created caused his training to kick in, and he raised his rifle to take aim.

****

The elevator doors opened. Automatic gunfire filled the room, spraying the rooster's blood and gore across the adjacent window. It fell to the floor with a huge WHOMP! in front of Rob. Its head turned and looked at him in that herky-jerky manner chickens have

23

when eyeing something. Even after taking over twenty .223 caliber rounds to its body, it still tried to get up. Its wings flapped in slow motion. Its hideous mouth gnashed about. The captain demanded the nurse-looking lady wheel Erma into the elevator and down to safety. Erma held up her hand to stop. She would not leave. Not yet.

"Take me to it," Erma said quietly. "I need to see it."

The nurse lady hesitated on shaky legs. Erma motioned with her hand to move her forward toward the beast. The nurse lady reluctantly complied.

"It's not safe, Cousin! It's not dead!" the captain interjected in Spanish and stepped into Erma's path. She motioned for him to move to the side with a sweep of her frail hand. Reluctantly, he also did as instructed. Slowly, her wheelchair approached the feathered heap. Erma stared into its large glowing eyes as it jerked its head to the side. It stared into hers in what seemed to be recognition. It stopped thrashing. Its chest heaved in anger as pink fluid oozed from its beak. Their eyes stayed locked together. Images from that night in 1970 played in her mind, the night she and her husband Joe, with their two small kids, Annie and Tommy, were terrorized by that demonized abomination, Colonel Sanders, also a white-and-black feathered rooster. Her own body was nearly ripped apart. She lost her ring finger in the melee that ensued. Tommy, her son, literally walked through a sea of glass that shredded the soles of his feet to bits. Her sweet Joe was savagely injured yet still saved their lives, but later was arrested and railroaded by law enforcement. The prosecuting attorney never believed what really happened and wanted a scapegoat. Who would believe it was crazed chickens that did all that to them? It was quite outlandish on the face of it. The simple-minded judge deemed Joe a psycho that tried to kill Erma and their two children. Joe was sentenced to fifty years in a supermax prison, where he later died from cancer.

Erma and the demonized rooster stared at each other a beat longer with equal hatred in their gaze. Then from under the faded blanket on Erma's lap, her hands slightly shaking, she took out a Taurus Judge pistol. Audible gasps were heard around her. The gun was loaded with three-inch magnum .410-gauge buckshot. She leveled it just a foot from the freak's face. Her shaking turned firm, resolute. Her eyes burned like smoldering embers. A faint smile played on her lips.

She squeezed the trigger. BOOM!

The hand cannon was deafening in the room. The recoil of the blast nearly threw the gun from Erma's hand. The beast's head exploded into a pink mist, leaving just a bloody stump of neck as its body spattered against the floor. Slowly she replaced the warm-barreled weapon under her blanket. She stared at the bloody creature a few seconds longer. Death nerves slowly opened and closed its talons a couple times each. Then its entire body lay still. Blood pooled around the carcass.

Satisfied, Erma motioned with her knotted hand for her nurse to come take her away. She turned to Rob and Mel as they emerged from under the table.

"My loves, I am tired. I need to lie down for a spell, rest this old body," she said ever so softly. The nurse-looking lady, in a hurry to leave the bloody room, turned Erma's chair and quickly wheeled her into the elevator. That smile still played on Erma's lips as the elevator doors slid shut.

Chapter Three

Flight 1245 from London passed over the Great Lakes headed for Dallas/Fort Worth Airport. Dr. Ernest Simms sat in the dark first-class cabin hunched over his laptop. He typed furiously on its keys and flicked his finger across its trackpad. He only had another couple hours to finish his report before the plane landed. Upon landing he was to turn his report over to the United States Department of Agriculture representatives that would be there to meet him. In the corner of his screen he noted it was just after 10:00 PM local time. Several passengers and a flight attendant were peering out of the windows at the huge brilliance of the supermoon in the sky. Dr. Simms paid no attention and kept clacking away on his keyboard. A fifty-year supermoon would certainly interest him any other night, but his work was much more important this particular one. Or so he thought.

Just weeks before, he had a breakthrough in his experimental work in a small town outside of London. It was such an important breakthrough that the USDA was paying him a lot of money to fly into Texas to meet them. Dr. Simms was the world's foremost expert on breeding the *Apis mellifera*, better known as the honeybee. Many years ago, thirty-one to be exact, the Africanized honeybee had taken over the bee population in South America and now recently the southern region of Texas. They wiped out over 80 percent of the domestic honey bee variety. This decline has led to major crop failures of fruit orchards, as honeybees play a huge role in their pollination, not to mention a huge hit to the multi-billion dollar honey industry. Africanized honeybees are not efficient pollinators and eat most of their own honey, leaving little for human production. Fruit farming and beekeeping makes up most of the agriculture in that region of the country. So the USDA had been working hard to find ways to get rid of them. Another negative aspect of the Africanized honeybee is their ill-temperedness and deadly swarm attacks on humans and animals. When their hive is provoked they send out five times the number of soldiers to relentlessly attack the threat. This has earned them the street name *killer bees*.

Where did they come from? Brazil, thirty-one years ago by him and his now nemesis, Dr. Warwick Kerr. Dr. Simms thought they were working on creating a more robust honeybee variety. No single insect directly benefits humans as much as the honeybee, and their numbers had been sharply declining the previous decade. So when he joined Kerr's group of concerned environmentalists called the Planet's Keepers in Brazil to use breeding as a way to halt the decrease in the honeybee population, he felt it was a noble pursuit to benefit the environment and mankind.

Their experiments consisted of crossbreeding European varieties with the African subspecies *Apis mellifera scutellata*. However, the result wasn't as they hoped. The new hybrid species was less useful in the way of pollination and honey making and much more aggressive. Much, much more. Dr. Simms knew they must destroy the hybrid hives and their bees. When Kerr and the Planet's Keepers learned of the new bee's capabilities, they refused to allow their destruction. Dr. Simms couldn't understand why and adamantly opposed their decision to continue cross-breeding. Under duress and threat, he continued the experiments under the supervision of Kerr directly. The Planet's Keepers now seemed keen on weaponizing the bees to target those with dissenting viewpoints of their global environmental agendas.

Dr. Simms staged an explosion in his lab late one night and escaped. However, inadvertently, twenty-six swarms of the Africanized bees escaped too. Since then, they had blown through every warm, humid, low-altitude community like a motorcycle gang, raping, pillaging, and fouling the honeybee gene pool in their wake.

Later he learned the Planet's Keepers were constantly mucking with science in the name of the environment for all sorts of global ecological extortion schemes. In Dr. Simms's opinion, Dr. Warwick Kerr and the Planet's Keepers needed to be stopped. But he knew that was impossible, as they were now the world's foremost environmentalist group and well-funded by most global leaders, both in the government and private sectors. He and the Planet's Keepers were a news darling being doted on by every celebrity in Hollywood. They had the support of all the social media platform owners, allowing their brand of "green thinking" to become the most mainstream religion out there, quashing all dissenting views.

Dr. Simms read over the last of his report. Satisfied, he took a deep breath. His latest discovery found DNA sequences responsible for aggressive behaviors, pollination habits, and honey production in the Africanized bee's genome. But further, he discovered they could be positively modified relatively easily using his new breeding technique. If these new modified bees were fostered into the overall bee population, his studies showed that the amazing virtues of the honeybee could be restored, eliminating the Africanized strand for good. Take that, Warwick Kerr. He smiled to himself, and then his thoughts turned to hoping his test subjects were faring well in the cargo hold of the plane. Transporting them could be tricky due to the FAA rules for transporting bees in general. Even with the wavers he secured from the USDA, the container seemed very restrictive on air flow. Oh well, he really just needed a few to survive, and he was sure that would happen.

He flagged down the flight attendant and ordered vodka and club soda. He put his Bose headphones on, synced them to his phone, and fit them over his ears. He pulled up his music app and hit Play. The soothing saxophone jazz of Labron Dennis relaxed his mind. He then reclined his seat and rubbed his tired eyes as he laid his head back to rest.

****

"Well, hell. I'm gonna piss my damn pants," Paul Carson muttered to his wife. She looked up crossly at him from the romance novel she was reading on her Kindle. She hated to be interrupted when the trashy parts got her juices flowing. For the last twenty minutes her husband had been trying to get to the toilet while she had been anticipating this graphic chapter. The two main characters finally had the chance to debaucherously one-up the other.

"Oh! It's free." He jumped out of his seat only to see another passenger casually stand with their small child and walk into the toilet. Click. Occupied. Paul returned to his seat, cursing under his breath.

"If you don't go and stand by the restroom door . . ." his wife said, very put out now, unable to tear her eyes from the filthy words displayed on her Kindle. Each time he stood up, another passenger further up the plane got ahead of him.

"Last time I did that, the flight attendant reminded me that's against policy and made me sit back down. And why did you have to book our seats all the way back here? I swear they are putting diuretics in the ginger ale," he kept on. "Aww, damn, I just peed a little," he said, now squirming.

"Go stand by the door and refuse to sit down. Now go!" his wife demanded, then shoved him into the aisle with a murderous look in her eyes. Finally, he relented and went to wait by the door. Just as he arrived, the lock clicked, which made the sign show vacant, and the door opened. He rushed inside, bumping into the guy coming out.

"Sorry!" Paul said, and quickly entered the toilet, not even locking the door. He barely had his zipper down before his deluge let go. He took several deep breaths as his burning bladder began to ease. Inches from his head he thought he heard a buzzing noise. He looked up at the air vent, and there was a bee crawling out of it. But it looked strange. Its head was more bulbous and appeared to have a ring of small spikes around it. Its wings were smaller than a normal bee's, and he briefly wondered how it flew with them. Oh, and something about its legs. How many did bees usually have? But it was the long, sharp stinger coming from its tail that caused him to think he might wanna finish his business sooner rather than later.

"What the hell is a bee doing in . . . ?" but before he could finish his sentence, the hideous creature flew up his nose. Paul slapped his face and felt the buzzing of its wings moving quickly up into his nasal cavity. He felt the first sting between his eyes. He screamed in pain and fell out of the unlocked door, spilling into a beverage cart as it was being wheeled by. The cart fell on the flight attendant, who went down hard with a crash. Paul continued smacking his face as blood gushed from his nose. He shoved his entire finger into his nostril, clawing for the insect. His pants were now around his ankles, and piss was hosing down the passengers around the bathroom as he tripped and slammed his face into an armrest.

Paul's wife was doing some squirming of her own now. The most vulgar adjectives the author could use coupled with many gyrating verbs described the unbridled fornication between the two characters and had her body on fire. Thankfully, the chapter ended as she exhaled. She was flush and sweating, wishing she was on the receiving end of that gorgeous stud's probing efforts. She closed her eyes and looked up, feeling his strong hands pulling her against his chiseled torso. A cool breeze of a flight attendant running past stirred her from her fantasy. She heard some yelling toward the front of the plane. She opened her eyes and realized Paul hadn't returned to his seat. People were standing now, watching something unfold ahead of them. She raised herself onto a knee to see for herself over the crowd. In the front of the plane several people were swatting and slapping the air around them while others screamed and clawed at their faces.

"What's happening?" she asked a man in front of her, but he ignored her with wide eyes. Then she heard several murmurs about terrorists. This caused mass panic as people scrambled toward where she sat in the back of the plane.

****

Dr. Simms rested comfortably in his first-class seat. He wondered where the flight attendant was with his drink. That made him think about his bees and if they were thirsty too. Wait, did he bring their nectar? They would need a shot of it as soon as they landed. In his hurry to make it to the airport, he couldn't remember if he'd packed it or not. He picked up his backpack from under the seat in front of him and unzipped its flap. Concerned, he reached inside and rummaged around. Finally, his hand found the familiar tube and pulled it out. The emerald-and-ruby label read Bee Nectar. In the label's corner was the logo of the Chow company, and underneath it read, Quality Pet Supplements Since 1968, he breathed a sigh of relief and dropped it back in his bag. From the air vents bees continued filling the cabin of the plane, relentlessly attacking anything that moved.

Moments later the captain opened the cockpit door clawing his bloody face and screaming incoherently. Dr. Simms's eyes jerked open, and he looked into the open cockpit door. Behind the frantic captain, sprawled over the center console, was the copilot. His head was so swollen, his facial features looked like they were drawn onto a balloon. Dr. Simms felt the plane's nose begin to drop rapidly until nearly straight down. The sound of a rushing throng of screaming people came rushing toward him. He removed his headphones and looked back just as all the unbuckled passengers, loose luggage, beverage carts, and anything else not bolted down from the back of the plane joined him in the front of the plane. Crushing him.

Chapter Four

The sun began to peek over the horizon. The captain ordered everyone out of the conference room. It was obvious now that it was not safe. Technicians and officers packed up their belongings and made their way down the elevator in small groups. Mel and Rob were herded into the elevator with an officer the captain had asked to escort them. The escort inserted a security badge into a card reader, then pushed an unmarked button on the panel.

"Where will that button take us?" Mel asked.

"To the access tunnels leading to our central bunker," he replied.

"Nice," she said sarcastically, exhaling loudly. Rob took her hand and gave it a comforting squeeze. When they were kids, Mel had always been a little claustrophobic, and to this day, she still hated small areas.

Being in elevators was bad enough, always thinking, what if it stalls and gets stuck between floors? Her pulse quickened with that thought now as the doors closed. When she was about five years old, their mother threw Rob a birthday party. He didn't have any real friends, as he was kind of a loner. So to give him a somewhat normal party experience, his parents invited some random kids of other parents they knew from their country club. Rob and Mel's family lived on a small farm. Their father had started a chicken-hatching endeavor aside from his day job as a marketing executive and had all sorts of things that lent to that effort lying around. A couple of the boys found an old wash tub he used for hatching chicks and shoved Mel underneath it. They sat on top of it laughing and wouldn't let her out. Rob wasn't there when they put her under it, but shortly after they trapped her, he came outside to tell everyone it was time for cake and ice cream. When he saw them sitting on the tub taunting Mel and heard her screaming for her life underneath it, he ran to her and shoved them off. One of the boys shoved Rob to the ground. Mel was red-faced as she exploded from under the tub. Tears streamed down her face. Grass and leaves clung to her hair. Instead of running into the house for her mommy like most girls that age would do, she lunged at the boy that had shoved Rob and socked him right in the mouth. His lip busted wide and turned his teeth bright red. Instead, it was him that ran into the house calling for his mommy. She then took off after the other one, but he ran away and was too fast. From then on they celebrated birthdays with only their own family.

More recently she was confined to a small stainless steel–lined room in the back of a massive black bus. While in there a drug cartel kingpin murdered the closest guy she ever had to a boyfriend while he stood beside her pleading, trying to clear her of any wrongdoing. Jimmy was shot through his left eye as an example of what happened when you screwed up working for that cartel. But karma had done justice just before she arrived in this compound yesterday evening. She had gotten to watch that huge black bus explode into a massive fireball, killing the cartel boss in what she hoped was a hideously torturous death.

The elevator stopped, and the doors slid open. Ahead was a long hallway. It was brightly lit and looked like a hallway in any above-ground type of building. Had she not known she was underground, she probably never would have guessed. In her mind she figured it was dirt walls and floors, bare light bulbs hanging from wooden timbers acting as trusses, like in a coal mine. She breathed a bit easier, softening her anxiety as their escort led them forward. There weren't many doors off the hallway, and the few she saw were solid and closed. However, one had a window in it, and she peered through it. Inside was a workout center complete with free weights, several machines, and treadmills. Toward the back was a mat surrounded by mirrors on the walls for sparring martial arts. Both a speed bag and heavy bag hung beside the space. She must come back later when things settled down to blow off some steam. Maybe later that night before bed, then a hot shower to help her sleep.

They rounded a corner, and through another door they could see an empty cafeteria with snack and soda vending machines colorfully lit in the darkness. Finally, they came to a set of frosted glass doors. The escort scanned his security card and pushed through them. They opened to another conference room like in the control tower, but much larger and with more plush seats. It was already buzzing with activity that continued from before that freak of science burst through the glass wall in the tower.

"Please take a seat wherever you like. Breakfast will be brought in soon. After that I will show you to your quarters," said the escort. Rob and Mel took a seat in some theater-style chairs. On the wall opposite their seats was a bank of several huge LED flatscreens.

"Here." The escort handed Mel a remote control similar to the ones she'd used before, just slightly thicker. "Use the arrow buttons to move that colored square around whichever section you want to hear, and the sound will play." Mel used the arrow keys to highlight a newscast, and instantly she heard a foreign language commentary through the speakers above them. Seeing she had the gist of the remote, he joined the throng of other officers conversing in groups here and there. Like in the control tower, some LCD screens were sectioned into squares, each showing a different news broadcast from around the world with muted sound until she highlighted them with the colored square.

Other screens appeared to be rotating camera feeds from around the compound. The footage was of different aspects of the Lockdown Protocol being underway, which they both found interesting. Some were of the fire brigade stowing trucks, hoses, and other things from the cleanup of the black bus explosion. Another showed the bus being towed on a huge 18-wheeler flatbed. It was now just a charred hull of twisted scrap metal, no longer menacing and intimidating. Mel smiled inwardly at that as she worked the remote and moved the colored square from section to section until she heard English over the speakers. It was from a blonde woman reporter in that deadpan voice serious reporters try to intone. She was standing with her back to a line of law enforcement officers all dressed in full riot gear. From time to time she peered over her shoulder, fearful as gunshots and screams filled the air around her. It clearly wasn't safe for her to be there. It made Mel wonder why reporters put their lives in harm's way like that. It must add to the authenticity of the situation they reported on, she thought as she listened in to what the reporter was saying:

"The scene behind me is being played out all across the country in small communities and major cities alike. People are terrified. Family pets are turning on their owners, viciously killing entire households. Non-domestic animals are turning farms and rural communities into bloodbaths. Scientists are baffled at what has triggered animals to mutate into these machines of mayhem that seem to be targeting mostly humans. Already the death tolls are reaching into the hundreds of thousands. Hospitals are filling up, and law enforcement is fully taxed, quickly becoming exhausted. Many are fleeing their ranks to get home to their families. Looters are in full force, taking advantage of the anarchy in the streets, risking their lives for anything they can get their hands on. I'm Tiffany Cross, reporting live amidst the carnage of what is now being called an animal apocalypse. Back to you in the studio, Eddie."

The term *animal apocalypse* was used time and time again as Mel flipped the channels. Each one showed the same helpless people being slaughtered. Even though she couldn't understand the words, she could sense the universal panic and desperation in the videos and pictures being displayed. With no apparent end to the violence and killing on what seemed like every corner of the planet, she felt very fortunate that she and Rob were together underground behind the high walls outside. Thanks to her grandmother, the Rurales had them well protected.

Mel heard breakfast being wheeled in on several carts. Each was topped with shiny dome lids. Another cart came in last with a stack of plates, glasses, and silverware. Three Mexican women began lifting lids and preparing juice and coffee. The smell filled the room quickly and caused an impromptu line to form, awaiting the signal to proceed buffet style. Rob had drifted off again, but Mel was alert and watching the LCD monitors closely. She realized she hadn't eaten since grabbing fast food at a Whataburger when they left Dallas the day before. Her stomach growled, and she felt guilty seeing the helplessness on the news and now feeling hungry. But hunger was a powerful force regardless of the situation. She nudged her snoozing brother as she stood to join the others in line. Rob stirred but laid his head back and continued his slumber. A couple minutes later she sat back next to him with a plate piled high with fresh warm corn tortillas sitting atop a huge helping of huevos rancheros with two fried eggs, refried beans, and salsa. She knew she wouldn't eat it all, but at the rate the scrumptious grub was disappearing from the food carts, Rob was certainly going to miss out. So she grabbed some extra on her plate for him when he awoke. She dove into the amazing meal. It was the first home-cooked one she had eaten in ages. The fried eggs popped their sunny-side-up pockets and spread creamy yellow yolk all over the egg whites, chorizo, and potatoes underneath. Scooping it up into the fresh tortillas, she savored each bite. She soon realized Rob was going to be shit outta luck on getting any. You snooze, you lose, big bro. Oh well, she did see those vending machines back in that breakroom. She hoped he had some loose change on him.

****

The breakfast dishes had been cleared, and everyone was back to business coordinating Rurales assets around Mexico trying to combat the animal mutations and protect the public. It wasn't going very well. The civilian death toll in Mexico was exponentially growing, too fast to keep up with, and the Rurales had now lost nearly fifty of their own in the last six hours. They weren't a large outfit on the whole and were considering retreating before they were effectively wiped out. All across the globe it was no different as Mel watched the news footage. She wondered what CIA agent Benjamin Masters and his sidekick Scott were doing. They were the ones that directed Mel and Rob to Mexico in the first place in hopes of finding their grandmother. They found her, but hadn't heard anything from the duo since.

Around her she heard a commotion. Several officers gathered around her and Rob and were watching the LCD footage from security cameras around the small landing strip. Rob woke up at the ruckus in time to see a sleek titanium gray helicopter glistening brightly from the morning sun as it whizzed by one of the cameras. The captain pushed his way through the group and barked an order in Spanish. An officer grabbed a control pad with a joystick that controlled the camera and began tracking the aircraft but struggled. It banked hard and circled the control tower at very high speed, narrowly missing it. Mel had never seen a helicopter move so quickly and turn on a dime like that. She thought she could hear its rotors thumping above her but couldn't tell if it was her imagination or not.

"Our airspace is a no-fly zone! Find out who that is and prepare defense measures!" barked the captain. Several officers got on cell phones, some calling to the tower to hail the pilot, and others calling the perimeter guards ordering the readiness of anti-aircraft ordinance.

"Where did it go?" asked the officer with the control pad. The footage on the LCD was panning in all directions, but no sleek chopper was to be seen. It was too fast to track with the cameras. By the time the camera found the chopper, it had landed on the helipad.

"Our perimeter guards are locked on the target. It just landed," reported an officer.

"Are the trespassers armed?" the captain asked.

"We can't tell. Several are exiting the chopper."

"Hold a bead on them. If they show aggression, shoot them where they stand," the captain ordered through gritted teeth.

"The tower has the pilot on the radio. He claims they are from the US government," yelled one of the officers to the captain. The captain was furious. *US government or not, they can't just invade sovereign air space like that*, he thought to himself.

"I don't give a damn! Stand down defense measures and take them into custody. I want them brought straight to me!" he ordered.

Moments later the glass doors opened. Several guards spilled into the room with rifles at the ready. Officers around the conference room placed hands on the butts of their service pistols. Mel wondered if she should grab Rob and duck under the table again. Rob couldn't see the trespassers through the commotion until the guards moved aside before the captain. He froze in disbelief. Then a strange relief washed over him and a huge smile spread across his face. In the center of the guards was Dr. Sheltie, Scott, and someone he didn't recognize. Both Dr. Sheltie and Scott looked a little green around the gills. The other man stood nonchalantly in a cowboy hat, vigorously chewing gum. The three were led by a tall, rugged-looking man with a thick mop of salt-and-pepper hair—Benjamin Masters.

Chapter Five

"Why you reckless son of a bitch!" the captain yelled in English and advanced quickly toward the tall, rugged man. No one expected this reaction from the captain, as he was generally cool mannered, but everyone could easily see he was spitting mad about this group's unannounced presence. A couple of officers drew their guns slowly in anticipation. Rob cringed, foreseeing the large captain smash Masters in his face with his fist. Masters held his arms open in surrender, but the captain still stomped forward. Just when Rob knew he would swing a right hook, they embraced, loudly slapping each other on the back.

Rob and Mel traded a confused look. The two men pulled apart, still holding each other by the shoulders. They spoke in excited, joyous Spanish, then hugged again. Rob was glad to see each and every person around him staring, just as confused. The captain swatted down the guards' rifles around them and turned to the room.

"Everyone! It is fine. It is just an old compadre. No need to be alarmed," he said, grinning wide.

"Come, Ben. Join me in my office. Bring your friends," the captain said, motioning toward the other three and then toward Rob and Mel. Still in shock they walked through the crowd out the doors. Ahead of them the captain and Masters continued their joyous conversation in Spanish. Rob sidled up beside Dr. Sheltie and expressed his relief that she was OK. She hooked her right arm around him and gave him a hug as they continued walking.

"And you must be Mel?" she said, looking across Rob as Mel walked beside him.

"Yes, ma'am," she answered. Dr. Sheltie released Rob's waist, then went to Mel and hugged her hard around her neck. Mel looked puzzled at Rob over Dr. Sheltie's shoulder.

"I am so glad you are OK. I've been worried sick about you," Dr. Sheltie said, releasing her.

"Thank you?" Mel said, puzzled, and gave Rob a side-eye. He just shrugged at her and they continued walking. Then Mel's gaze fell onto Scott, the techy CIA guy that seemed like more than just a computer nerd. After he defended them against the cartel thugs and then helped them across the border the previous night, he had crossed her mind more than a few times. He was just ahead of her, and their eyes met briefly as they entered the hallway. Her heart fluttered, and it frustrated her because she couldn't control it. He walked in a casual but powerful step. He wasn't tall, but she could tell he was fit and light on his feet. She tried not to notice how well his jeans fit under the light jacket he wore. Ever since they met in that abandoned house back in McAllen, Texas, she felt drawn to him for some reason. Inside she was excited to see him, but she kept her face neutral as she recalled his good-natured personality and dry humor. Not the macho bullshit she was used to.

She had really poor luck with men, mostly because during the last several years she ran a waypoint for drugs and prostitutes for the cartel. So most of the men she encountered were either johns or thugs. She had very little experience around truly good guys and never had a meaningful relationship. Only transactional encounters. Jimmy was the closest thing to someone she had feelings for. She never could define those feelings, but she knew it wasn't love. Even after she witnessed his brains blown out in the back of that bus, she didn't really miss him. She didn't even think she cried for him. Mostly, she just felt sorry it happened. But in the end, glad it was him and not her. Feeling that, she might feel bad just a little. No, she didn't. Definitely glad it wasn't her.

The group stopped outside of the elevator. The doors opened, and the captain stood aside and let his guests enter first. Scott entered before Mel and turned. They met eyes again. Scott's blue. Mel's emerald green. He smiled at her as she entered and stood next to him.

"I'm glad to see you are OK," he said, looking over at her. The rest of the group entered, and the doors closed. She could feel his shoulder against hers. She felt warm all of a sudden.

"Thank you. It's good to see you made it OK, too," she said softly, looking quickly over at him and then down to the center of the captain's back in front of her as he and Masters still chit-chatted in Spanish. The doors opened back in the foyer of the control tower. Mel exited and realized she had never once thought about the elevator stalling and so many people crammed together, stuck between floors. At least Scott was good for that, keeping her sane during elevator rides. Seemed with him she was always at ease. Felt safe. Even with bullets whizzing around her.

They exited the control tower, and a large desert-tan-colored, heavily armored Chevrolet Suburban sat idling. The driver stood beside and held the captain's door open. Once the captain was secured inside, the driver circled the vehicle, helping everyone else in. He then climbed in behind the wheel and shifted the armored beast into drive. It took several minutes, then the SUV stopped in front of an elaborate building. Rob recognized it when they first arrived in the compound the previous night. However, the windows and all doors had steel mesh over them now. This must have been a Lockdown Protocol protection measure. After the event earlier this morning in the control tower, he was glad to see the fortification efforts around the glass doors and windows.

****

Everyone was seated around the spacious office with the captain behind his desk. No joyous chit-chat now. Just somber, serious conversation.

"So when Annie called me that a huge black bus was trying to ram her car off the road, her cousin Raul took one of our armored vehicles out to help her. I knew that bus was Jefe Manuel, and I knew they were in grave danger. He was a crazy killer. Raul was able to destroy the bus," the captain elaborated further into the events from the previous night that brought Mel and Rob to La Casa Ballerinas.

"Was Raul hurt?" Rob asked, concerned.

"Yes. He is in our infirmary recovering from several broken bones, a few burns, and a concussion. But he will recover fully."

"We owe him our lives," Mel said next, also concerned.

"He is grateful you three were unharmed," the captain said, then turned back to Masters. "We shuttled Rob and Mel into the compound just as the supermoon went into position. We don't know why it caused these animal mutations, but Prima Erma knew it might happen again from her experience fifty years ago. She convinced the then Rurales captain to create the Lockdown Protocol," the captain explained to the group. "Many didn't believe her. Only a child's fairy tale . . . until it actually happened. Now it is the world's worst nightmare," he said grimly.

"Well, old friend, here is what we know," said Masters, speaking English for the first time since arriving. He proceeded to explain the weaponization of the animal feed by the CIA with the Chow company, the far-reaching popularity of the Chow brand all across the world and how the genetically modified ingredients were still in use today, and how the moon tied into it as the catalyst for the horrible events of the night by having the government-planted device on its surface that triggered the mutations in the animals. He kept a few details to himself, Rob noticed.

"What do you suspect we do, amigo?" the captain asked.

"We need our gear from the chopper. Sheltie and Scott need a place to work with internet access while the world still has it," he said, but not jokingly. The captain picked up his phone and barked some Spanish at the person on the other end and then hung up.

"I have someone coming to take you to the chopper, then to a workspace—" He was interrupted as the door burst open and a teenaged boy, about sixteen, quickly approached the captain's desk.

"Grandfather, why are you ignoring my calls? We must help Ariana's village!" he exclaimed with tears in his eyes.

"I told you we will, and we will. You cannot burst in here like this. I am very busy. Now go!" the captain scolded the boy.

"If you will not help, then I will go and help them myself!" the boy said before turning and storming out.

"My apologies. That's my grandson, Diego. He is worried about his girlfriend and her village. We have armored convoys patrolling the countryside and assisting where needed, but we haven't gotten to her yet, and our resources are getting slim. I am not sure we will get to them at all. The morale of my team is receding, and I can't blame them. With our losses rising . . ." He broke off and took a deep breath, then turned toward the mesh-covered window before returning his gaze to Masters. "They have families they are worried about too," the captain said, genuinely sorry and feeling helpless. He rubbed his eyes with the heels of his hands and stood, exhaling loudly.

"Let's get you guys settled in for the evening," he said. He motioned one of their armed escorts into the room from the hall. The captain spoke rapidly in Spanish to the escort, then turned to the group and said, "Please go with Pedro. He will show each of you to an area where you can regroup with the internet and secure comms, then to your quarters."

Masters thanked him, and they filed out of the captain's office. They were led to a small conference room back in the underground bunker, and the escort explained how to access the internet and use the communication equipment. After that, he led them to the barracks a bit further down the long hallway. There were bunks and a seating area inside a small kitchenette. The escort explained there were basic food and drink provisions for them in the refrigerator and cabinets. He then opened a closet door for storage and another leading into what looked like a locker room with stalls for toilets and showers. He apologized that there wasn't a separate area for the women, but to date the Rurales only had men in their ranks. Mel just shrugged and set her pack on a lower bunk, claiming it as her own.

"I shared a room with two brothers growing up. I'm good," said Dr. Sheltie as she tossed her pack on the bed above Mel. The others took empty bunks and began settling in. It had been a long day, and each welcomed some much-needed shut-eye.

Chapter Six

Mel awoke suddenly. It took her a second to recall where she was until she heard all the snoring. Images of Jimmy's bloody body crumpling to the floor of the stainless steel room in the back of the cartel boss's bus were fresh in her mind. She thought she felt her ears still ringing from the gunshot. She would be forever grateful that Rob figured out how to contact her to meet him in that motel a couple nights ago. It was careless and beyond dangerous, but it had allowed her a chance to escape what she may not have otherwise. She checked her phone. It was 1:30 a.m. She had been asleep for only a few hours. In the dark she could make out Masters below Rob in the bunk across from her. Next to them she could see the chopper pilot that she now knew as Scooter, on the top bunk, but the bottom was empty. Scott's bunk.

She slowly slid out of her bed and stood, then walked to the locker room door. Part of her hoped he might be in there and she might get a glimpse of him bare. The thought warmed her as she slipped into the room. Nothing. Just the dripping of a leaky shower head echoing in an empty stall. Aggravation at herself for having such thoughts snuffed out her flushed senses. Why did thoughts of him do that to her? No guy had ever stirred such feelings in her. She needed to work out some aggression, get control of her hormones. She recalled the gym back down the hall when they entered the bunker area. Perfect. It had been a while since she had worked out in a decent gym. For the last month she was forced to use what passed for a gym in the Dallas county jail. It wasn't exactly to her standards. She needed a heavy bag to work out her long, lean limbs. To feel its canvas cover smack against her feet and knuckles as she dished out an ass whipping.

She slipped out of the locker room back into the bunk area and quickly put on some workout clothes provided to her. Of course they were for men—the typical gray colored cotton T-shirt and matching shorts that had been laundered a thousand times. They reminded her of junior high gym class. Back then her body failed to fill them out during her early stages of puberty. Now she had all the shapely curves of a grown woman, but the clothes being three sizes too large gave her the sense she was fourteen again. She tied the long shirt at her waist, giving her breasts a fighting chance of displaying her female identity. She quietly opened the door and entered the long hallway. Being underground, it was as silent as a tomb. Only a slight electrical hum could be heard from the night lights illuminating a path on the floor as she crept down the hall toward the gym. Approaching the door, she saw a shaft of light coming from within. Someone was in there. As she got closer, the sound of punches and kicks to a heavy bag could be heard.

Mel slowly approached the window and barely caught a glimpse of someone at the far end of the room. The heavy bag jiggled slightly from a recent assault. She wondered where the person had gone. Then a man quickly came into view delivering a hard round-house kick to the top of the bag, then twisted to deliver a bone-jarring elbow followed by several hard jabs before bouncing backward out of sight again. Mel's breath caught in her throat. It was Scott.

To pull off that move, Mel knew it took many years of experience in martial arts. She herself had nearly a decade of training in various disciplines. However, she mostly focused on Krav Maga, an extremely deadly form of martial arts created by Israeli commandos. Again she was amazed at his agility as he delivered another skilled combination of kicks and punches to the bag. As if sensing her presence, he looked over toward the door. Recognizing her through the window, he smiled. She clumsily waved with a flicking of her fingers. He laughed and motioned for her to come in. Her body warmed instantly, frozen in place. Her mind went numb as panic set in. She hadn't brushed her hair after waking up. The rest of her surely looked like hell after the long day before falling asleep without a shower.

I bet I stink, she thought, fighting the urge to sniff her armpits.

She glanced down at the slight stubble on her legs. She couldn't even recall the last time she'd shaved. Geez.

"What the hell is wrong with me?" she muttered to herself, feeling awkwardly self-conscious as she entered the gym. Scott wore the same gray cotton outfit as she did. However, his body filled it out like God intended it to be. Sweat soaked his T-shirt, and it clung to his cut chest and rippling abs. His shorts were pulled tight around his strong thighs above chiseled calves and bare feet.

Before she could inspect his body further, he exclaimed, "Come on in! Just trying to wear myself out so I can sleep. I'm all wound up."

"Yeah, I know what you mean," Mel replied, swallowing down her shyness. She needed to get her blood flowing, work up a sweat. Standing there like a gawking teenager was not her style, but around Scott it seemed all she knew how to do.

"Mind if I work on the bag for a second? Get my blood flowing?"

"Go for it. I'm gonna grab some water."

Scott turned to walk over to the water machine. He heard some punching as Mel warmed up. He leaned down to grab a paper cup and then filled it with water. Light snap punches filled the air behind. He thought they sounded sexy as he pictured Mel's lean legs flexing while supporting her tight body as she threw feminine jabs into the bag. He felt the urge to impress her. Maybe he'd let her hold the bag so she could feel his manly punches slamming into it. As he drained the last gulp of water, he heard a feral yell, and a huge *thump* made him jump in surprise, choking on the water. He turned in time to see the heavy bag break loose from the hook in the ceiling as it slid across the floor dragging its chain as Mel landed on her feet as elegant as a cat.

"Wow!" he exclaimed, his eyes wide with shock and disbelief.

"Sorry," she winced, acting apologetically. *That should get his attention*, she thought.

"No, I'm the one that's sorry," he said as he looked up and circled the broken hook in the ceiling.

"Why are you sorry?"

"I guess my workout must've loosened up the hinge up there. You could've been hurt."

Really? Mel thought he was joking but quickly could see he wasn't. The fact she had just applied enough leg force into that heavy bag to kill a person seemed lost on him, and that had her momentarily in disbelief.

"I've had the force of my punches measured on a PowerKube at about a hundred thousand units," he went on in a braggadocious tone.

No, please don't, Mel thought, utterly disappointed. *Please don't be a self-absorbed douchebag too.*

Seems all men she came across were so impressed with themselves. She hoped Scott was different. But the more he talked, the worse it got. Mel's blood pressure shot up and her temper flared. She tuned out what he was saying but could see his jaw still spewing macho bullshit, something she absolutely couldn't stand in a man. What a prick.

"They really need to consider letting the girls . . ."

Wait a minute . . . the girls?

" . . . have their own padded section . . ."

Padded section?

". . . to protect them . . ."

Protect them!

That was all Mel could take. She curled her lip and lunged forward to land an overhead six to his face in hopes of shutting up his misogynistic regurgitation. Just before her fist connected with his jaw, he quickly pulled back. Following her momentum, he grabbed her wrist and twisted her to the floor. He attempted to roll her into an arm bar, but she countered by wrapping him in her long, strong legs. Now he had her in a full guard with her back on the ground. He pinned her wrists over her head. He wore a playful smirk, thinking he had her bested. But little did he know this was all her plan.

"Do you give?" he said, breathing heavily into her face. He was stronger than her, but she now knew she had better training.

Catching him off-guard, underestimating her own strength and quickness, she instantly freed her wrists. With her left hand she grabbed the back of his head at the crown, pulling his face hard against her chest. Then with her right arm, she performed a twelve to six elbow strike, causing him to scream in pain. Mel knew that this move, if done without expert precision, could paralyze him. Had she been really trying to hurt him, she would have shattered his clavicle and then slammed a second elbow at the base of his neck. Game over. Instead she landed her elbow into the crook of his neck and shoulder, momentarily paralyzing him, then swung herself around onto his back. From there she put him into a rear naked choke hold, inverting his spine and cutting off his oxygen. Scott was dazed and choked in pain. She pressed the side of her face to his.

"I never give," Mel hissed into his ear, spit flying from her lips.

Scott's vision was swirling as his oxygen was cut off. He started slapping his hands against the mat in the universal "I give up" signal. Mel held his throat in the crook of her elbow a couple seconds longer just to emphasize her point, then released him and moved off his back and stood. Scott rolled over, holding his neck and panting. The purple in his face subsided as he gulped in breaths of air.

"What just happened?" he said hoarsely, twisting his neck side to side. Thankfully nothing felt broken. He heard the door open and looked as he caught a glimpse of Mel leaving the gym, the door slamming behind her.

Chapter Seven

Off the coast of the southernmost tip of Argentina lies the Isla de los Estados, a small grouping of densely forested, mountainous islands. On these islands is the headquarters of the world's largest and most renowned environmentalist group, the Planet's Keepers. Sitting on a large deck that overlooked a lush, green valley, Dr. Warwick Kerr watched the sunrise. Several newspapers were stacked neatly on the table beside him, and one was open on the table in front of him. To his left were several LCD screens. On each were news broadcasts from all over the world. Each reported the same atrocities being committed by mutated killing machines across all the major cities on all continents. The world was in chaos. He had the volume of one channel broadcasting from the US.

"Groups of militias, survivalists, and thrill seekers alike have taken to the streets in many urban areas where the highest concentration of the mutant animals are being found, turning the streets into a real-life Hogan's Alley. I am here with a group calling themselves Beast Blasters. As you can see, these groups are arming themselves with para-military arsenals including high-power assault rifles, flamethrowers, and even grenade launchers for participating on a new online site. This site has created a home for a new sport called Kill Club, where players such as the Beast Blasters are streaming individual live feeds creating a first-person shooting experience with a real-time tally of confirmed kills. Fans can place bets on the site using Bitcoin and other cryptocurrency, with a percentage going to winning individuals and teams. There is also an area where online participants can build out their own fantasy kill team and participate in a league. Like during the time of the Roman Colosseum, the stakes are high. Many are risking death participating in this real first-person shooting craze, but even during apocalyptic times, people are finding ways to entertain and cash in. This is Tiffany Cross amongst the pandemonium. Back to you in the studio, Eddie."

Dr. Kerr leaned back and sipped his vanilla soy latte, basking in the deadly glow of the events at hand. It never ceased to amaze him how stupid humans had become. However, soon the planet would be rid of the human footprint, and Earth could heal and reward those dedicated to its preservation with a new Eden. Those that give lip service to saving the Earth because it was trendy and popular would soon be devoured by the beasts as they rampaged. If other stupid fools chose to have their deaths broadcast on the internet for fleeting entertainment, so be it. They'd all be dead soon enough. Mother Earth was dying. Man was killing her and had to be stopped. The Planet's Keepers had been working for decades on a plan to do just that. Dr. Kerr smiled widely as he watched that plan finally unfolding before his very eyes. If only his father could have been here to see this.

He thought back to 1973 , when his father, Franklin Kerr, came across the means for this elaborate plan. He founded the Planet's Keepers while in his junior year of college at Berkeley a decade earlier. Seeing the negative impact the World Wars had on the environment spurred him to take action with like-minded students.

Vietnam was ramping up, and he knew the taxing of this planet would be huge because of it. War strips the earth of its minerals to build all the war machines, weapons, and bullets. It sucks enormous amounts of oil from the Earth and then uses it to pollute the air. In some cases war ruins entire ecosystems for hundreds, maybe thousands, of years through atomic radiation in the deployment of bombs and in their testing. Man was a menace and hellbent on warmongering. The Planet's Keepers initially focused on war protests, as the concept of green environmentalists of today hadn't emerged yet. Franklin Kerr was a visionary and a charismatic leader. Within the first year they had over three hundred members across the United States and small groupings popping up in other countries.

Franklin Kerr's reputation grew. He entered into politics, becoming one of the first environmental lobbyists in Washington, DC. He became a huge thorn in the side of many politicians by being able to quickly organize outspoken and aggressive protests, especially during the election seasons for those not adopting some form of "Save the Earth" agenda. But where his biggest opportunity for the Planet's Keepers presented itself was in a meeting with the chairman of the Armed Services Committee. The chairman had put off Franklin Kerr as long as he could, until finally he decided if he met with Kerr before he was off to attend a re-election rally, then the Planet's Keepers being a disruption during it might be minimized. Threats had been made in the weeks leading up to his re-election rally. He figured he would give Franklin Kerr ten minutes and act as sympathetic to the environment as possible in hopes of a peaceful rally the next day. During the meeting with Kerr, one of the chairman's aides entered the office and delivered a file that had the Top Secret designation stamped on its cover. She instructed the chairman it was now OK to file and lock it away. Everyone had signed off on it.

The chairman opened the cover and gave it a quick glance and muttered to himself, "Big mistake shutting this down." He then looked across at Franklin Kerr and said dryly, "You may get what you want after all. Looks like the war could end soon. Hooray for the planet," he said dryly.

Franklin Kerr sat there puzzled, but before he could ask for clarity, the aide stuck her head in the door and asked the chairman if he had a minute to review something in the conference room. Franklin Kerr's pulse quickened as he stared at the Top Secret folder sitting on the desk in front of him. Was something inside it related to the Vietnam War coming to an end? He couldn't resist. Quickly he grabbed the file and opened the cover. What he saw, he didn't understand at first. Across the top of the front page was the title Supermoon Protocol. Below he read it was being canceled. He flipped more pages and read the name Operation Organic Death before seeing things about animal evolutions, lethal experiments, NASA's Apollo 11 mission in which a gamma-ray device was installed on the moon, with drawings and diagrams of the device followed by what looked like an astronaut work list. A highlighted paragraph explained that a retrieval and/or decommission of the moon catalyst device would be too costly. By leaving it active but ceasing the pet food weaponization, it should remain benign. Then he saw pages and pages of photos with some of the most gruesome scenes of humans ripped to pieces he had ever seen. A picture of a massively mutated dog, none like he had ever seen before, stood guard over a fresh corpse. Its eyes were large and had a faint golden glow to them. Its extended curled-up muzzle revealed row after row of razor-sharp teeth that made Franklin Kerr gasp. Then he saw the words, "The weaponization of animal feed by the Chow company." Next there were test results, complex recipes, and formulas. He didn't know why at the moment, but he tore out this section and stuffed it in his carryall bag. His gut told him this section was the crux of the whole thing . . . whatever it was. He tried to put the folder back on the desk as neatly as it was. He couldn't tell it was a few pages thinner, and hopefully the chairman wouldn't either. He quickly stood and left the office. Over the next week he studied up on the Texas-based Chow company and its emerging success, then how abruptly it was sold to an anonymous buyer in Maryland for an undisclosed amount of money. Franklin Kerr thought all of this sounded suspiciously like government intervention. Two days after his meeting with the chairman, the Paris Peace Accords were signed and the Vietnam war was over. So the chairman was right; the war *was* about to be over.

A month went by when Franklin Kerr was in a pub having beers with some of his fellow Keepers. On the television he saw a news reporter speaking and the Chow pet food company's logo in the upper corner. He shushed everyone and demanded the bartender turn up the sound. The reporter was explaining how one of the largest pet food companies in the US, the Chow company, was for sale due to bankruptcy. Franklin rushed out of the pub and went straight to his house and began calling a few of his most wealthy Planet's Keepers sympathizers. With funding, he was able to buy the flailing Chow company and interpret the information he took from that Top Secret file. From this, he put forth a diabolical plan to cleanse the world of mankind. The plan to continue the Supermoon Protocol for the next fifty years until the next supermoon appeared was hatched and the rest was history.

Dr. Warwick Kerr recalled his father telling him that story several times as a child, each time adding more context and detail as Warwick grew older and more mature. He continuously steeped Warwick in all aspects of his plan until he passed away five years ago. It was now up to Warwick to bring the Planet's Keepers into the new Eden—a world without human destruction, just pristine paradise. But what his father hadn't known was the larger plan Warwick himself had in motion alongside his father's plan, one that also involved the moon.

****

Masters awoke to his phone's alarm at 5:00 AM. He groggily stretched and sat up on the side of the bunk. He hadn't fully recovered from the previous months' sleep deprivation caused by a hideous nightmare that played out each time he closed his eyes. Like Rob, being relieved of it by Dr. Sheltie saved his sanity, but his body hadn't fully recovered yet. He took his phone and checked his messages. He saw he had a new voicemail. He hit play and put the phone to his ear. A man identifying himself as Trey Lett greeted him. Masters froze and held his breath. Trey Lett was the current National Intelligence Director, which was over the CIA— the same CIA that had been hunting both Rob and Masters up to this very second. The fact this was the voice of that man himself had him spooked. The message said:

"Masters, this is Trey Lett. I trust you know who I am and why I am calling you. I am requesting you come to DC and turn yourself in to me. Directly to me. I will arrange for this so you will be safe. Time is of the essence given what is happening in the world. I give you my word you will be treated fairly and have a chance to explain yourself to me directly. Oh yes, also bring with you Dr. Sheltie and Robert Florchett. We know they are with you. Call this number when you reach DC."

"What if it is a trap?" Rob asked, now sitting next to Masters on the bunk. In the top bunk across from them Dr. Sheltie was sitting, legs crossed, wiping the sleep from her eyes.

"I agree with Rob. What if it is a trap?" she said, then yawned.

"Yeah, I don't know. Given what is happening in the world, I doubt he would be wasting his time on a trap just for me," Masters answered. Mel rolled over in the bed underneath Dr. Sheltie's bunk and asked sleepily, "What trap? For who?"

"The National Intelligence director left a message on Masters's phone and wants him, me, and Dr. Sheltie to get to Washington, DC, immediately," Rob explained, but Mel hadn't heard him. Her attention was diverted to Scott's bunk, where he slowly sat up, working his neck back and forth, wincing in pain. For half a second she felt bad seeing him hurting, but then the details from their confrontation came to mind. No, she wasn't sorry. He'd gotten what he deserved.

Masters stood and went into the kitchenette to make some coffee. Rob lay back on his bunk. Scott stood and went into the locker room. He didn't look at Mel as he crossed by her. She could tell he was pissed, but she didn't care.

"I'm going down to that break room I saw down the hall to get a soda," said Dr. Sheltie as she slid off the top bunk.

"I'll join you," said Mel, following, eager to put some distance between her and Scott.

"Should I warm up the chopper, Boss?" Scooter asked as Masters passed him a cup of coffee.

"Not yet. I wanna talk to the captain first. He may need your help here once I explain your expertise to him. I'll see if he can spare a jet for us to get to DC."

"No problem. I'm gonna grab a quick shower and some grub," Scooter drawled as he stood with his coffee and walked into the locker room.

Scooter was all Texan, born and raised just outside of Ft. Worth. He walked like a Texan and he talked like a Texan. He was also slightly crazy in a Texan kinda way. Adrenaline was his drug of choice. He ran to danger like a glutton to an all-you-can-eat smorgasbord. He was arguably the best chopper pilot the US Marine Corps had ever produced. And his jet-flying skills weren't too far off either. He was recruited by the CIA five years prior after expressing his desire to retire from the service. The Marines just weren't challenging him enough anymore, and he was going into the private sector seeking more.

Now with the CIA, he pilots black ops missions and is their test pilot for new flying technology from the Defense Advanced Research Projects Agency, commonly known as DARPA. DARPA was established in 1958 and is an agency within the Department of Defense responsible for catalyzing the development of technologies that maintain and advance the capabilities and technical superiority of the US military. Many innovations in use today came from DARPA, things like GPS and the graphical user interface used on all popular computer systems today. They even invented the internet, then referred to as ARPANET, in 1968 as the foundation for an "intergalactic computer network" concept. More recently they invented what is now known as Siri. Yes, that Siri. Apple's digital virtual assistant started life as a DARPA project in the early 2000s, known as CALO. An acronym for Cognitive Assistant that Learns and Organizes. The research that spawned it originally focused on providing better technology to soldiers in the field via a technology that could learn from experience, take instructions, explain what it was doing, and reflect on the experience it just had. The CALO project lasted five years, from 2003 to 2008. Various technologies were spun out of it, including Siri, which was launched on the iOS App Store in February 2010 and acquired by Apple two months later. A year later, it was integrated into the iPhone 4s and is now a key part of Apple's device ecosystem.

Once inside the locker room, he saw Scott come from the showers wearing just a towel around his waist. Scooter noticed his neck was blooming with a nasty bruise.

"Oooh, looks like you got sandpapered really good," Scooter quipped. Scooter was known for his quips.

Scott covered the mark on his neck with his hand and said, "Just got a little rough in the gym, that's all. These Rurales are a tough bunch."

What Scooter couldn't see was that Scott's pride was far more black-and-blue than his neck. He hoped no one ever found out his beating had come from Mel. He wanted to be angry at Mel, but couldn't bring himself to be. He had thought about their encounter all night, lying in his bunk. He wasn't really sure what set her off to take that swing at his face. Whatever it was, he was going to be more careful around her. She was lethal with a temper and possibly off-center with everything going on around her. But even with that, he felt an attraction to her and hoped he hadn't blown his chances of getting to know her better.

The locker room door swung open and Masters stuck his head in.

"Meeting in the captain's office in ten minutes," he barked. He then eyed Scott a bit closer.

"What the hell happened to you?" Masters asked, indicating Scott's bruised neck.

Scott just exhaled loudly and looked up at the ceiling.

Chapter Eight

"You show real cojones, gringo," whistled the Rurales captain as he sat kicked back behind his desk. This was his reaction to Masters explaining Scooter's credentials, skills, and unclassified achievements, as well as a brief tale regarding aviation.

"Aww, shucks, man. It's the only talent God gave me, or I'd be about as useful as an eyeless needle," Scooter humbly drawled.

The captain chuckled at Scooter's way with words, then turned back to Masters. "Thank you, Ben, for offering his services to us. I have only one pilot left after two were killed and another deserted. I will instruct the one pilot left to fly you three to DC in my personal Gulfstream G450." Deserters in the Rurales ranks were becoming embarrassingly common. The Rurales force was down to a skeleton crew. Many had fled to their families.

"Thank you, amigo," Masters said to the captain. He then motioned to Rob and Dr. Sheltie. "Grab your gear and let's get in the air as soon as possible."

"What about us?" asked Mel, growing anxious. After so many years apart, she was scared if she and Rob separated, they may never see each other again. The world was too dangerous now, and she felt she needed to protect her brother.

"I need you, Scott, and Scooter to work with the captain's team here. Besides, my understanding is you can handle yourself deftly," Masters replied, giving Scott a knowing side-eye. Scott's face flushed as he tried not to react.

Masters continued, "Your abilities are more useful here, not in some bureaucrat's office in DC."

Mel had to agree with him about wanting to be in the action, and DC would be more suitably safe for Rob anyway.

"OK," she relented, and shot a glance over at Scott, wondering if he had cried to Masters about his ass whooping. Scott kept his eyes on Masters, wondering if he knew about their tangle in the gym. It never surprised him how Masters always seemed to know about everything.

The Gulfstream was fueled and idling on the tarmac when the Suburban pulled up. Everyone piled out, and those leaving grabbed their gear from the back and loaded it onto a luggage cart. Mel went to Rob.

"You be careful, big bro. If you need anything, call me." They hugged tight.

"You bet, Sis. Same for you," Rob said into her ear.

Dr. Sheltie walked over to them and said to Mel, "I hate we just met and I have to run. As soon as all this settles down, I can't wait to get to know you better."

Mel smiled and said that would be nice. She still was puzzled by Dr. Sheltie's keen interest in her and her attachment to Rob. It seemed almost paternal, but she couldn't put her finger on it. Seeing the two there chatting, Mel picked up on some subtle mannerisms they seemed to share.

Mel was yanked from her thoughts by Masters yelling, "Let's load up!" as he climbed up the stairs of the portable jetway. Mel and Rob hugged again, then Rob turned and jogged over to the stairs. At the top he turned and gave Mel a wave. She waved back, choked up, hoping this wasn't the last time she would see him. Her gut just knew things were soon going to get *muy loco* here in Mexico.

****

In the Suburban, Scott sat in the passenger seat, Mel and Scooter in the first bench row behind him. They watched the Gulfstream taxi over to the runway and throttle up. Then in an instant it was in the sky. Their driver got behind the wheel and closed his door. Without a word he put the vehicle in gear, and in silence they sped away back to the entrance to the bunker. Mel continued watching the jet grow smaller and smaller out her window when the truck's radio crackled to life in a barrage of Spanish. Then the driver's cell phone rang, and he answered it via Bluetooth over the truck's speakers. It was the captain. They all listened intently, not completely understanding. The captain was speaking fast and urgently.

Then the driver said in English while cutting the wheel hard left, "The captain needs your help right away." With that he punched the gas, and the huge Suburban squatted hard in the back, laying a trail of smoking rubber behind.

"What's going on?" Scott asked.

"The captain's nephew, Diego, has escaped the compound on his dirt bike. They think he is heading for his girlfriend's village," the driver replied as he slid the big vehicle around a turn.

"But worse, this morning the guard towers reported huge packs of wild mutated dogs on the main road. The captain is hoping Scooter can get up in his chopper to find Diego before those dogs do," the driver said, eyeing Scooter in the rearview mirror.

"You got it, Amigo," Scooter said in earnest.

They sped to the helicopter pad. Sitting there fully gassed up and ready was Scooter's pride and joy, a bullet-gray Sikorsky S-97 Raider. It was one of only three in existence, but the only one with huge modifications by DARPA. In its stock form, it was the second fastest military attack chopper in the world behind the Eurocopter X3. However, with DARPA's upgrades, this

S-97 handily beat the X3 in not just top speed but also agility and weapons payload. If Scooter ever had a child, this helicopter was it.

"My stomach is already doing flip-flops," Scott moaned as they slowed to a stop. Just seeing the chopper made him queasy. Scooter loved to push its limits for no good reason except, why not?

Scooter chuckled and reached up and patted Scott's shoulder, then looked at Mel and asked, "You ain't easily sickened by thrill rides, are ya?"

"Heck no. I love 'em!" she exclaimed as excitement bloomed across her face.

"Oooh, you don't understand," Scott said under his breath as he opened his door and slid off the seat. The helicopter was super sleek and nothing like any Mel had ever seen before. On top it had two rotors, the upper one being a few feet wider than the one below it. She noticed its tail was different too. Instead of the rear rotor being parallel to the tail, it was mounted perpendicularly on the rear like a propeller. The skin of the craft was so smooth, yet textured in certain places.

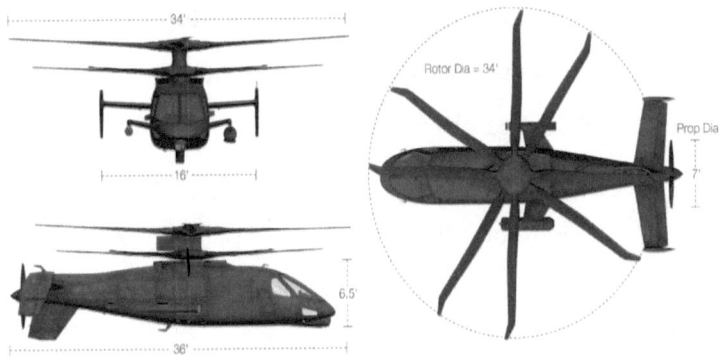

They exited the Suburban, and Scooter led them to the copter. He placed his palm against the side of the craft, and a door seemed to materialize out of nowhere as it slid smoothly open.

"Hop on in and grab a headset," he said cheerfully. He followed them in, and the door closed behind him. Inside, it was all business, rigged out for full commando transport. A bench seat along the back firewall and two double jump seats folded down behind the cockpit. On the wall next to the door were several controls and a touchscreen LCD display. Communication headgear was in custom charging units along the other wall. Scott took a headset and handed it to Mel and grabbed one for himself. Scooter's voice could be heard talking to the control tower as he was now settled into the pilot seat and working through the procedures to get in the air. A low hum resonated throughout the cabin, and Mel could see the props above begin to turn. Within just a minute they were spinning in a blur.

"Aight, boys and girls, I hope y'all are strapped in tight, 'cause this train's about to leave the station," Scooter drawled into his headset.

"Oh God," Scott muttered, closing his eyes. His knuckles were white from the death grip he had on his armrests. He didn't seem so macho now, Mel thought.

Suddenly, Mel was pressed down into her seat as her stomach sank hard to the floor. She wore a huge grin and squealed with excitement. In an instant she could see the entire compound below as the craft now tilted and threw her back against the back of her seat. She noticed the scorched earth where Jefe Manuel's huge black fortress of a bus exploded just two nights ago outside the compound's wall. Scrub grass and citrus trees were bent out in a perfect circle, the center black and charred.

The sheer power of the modified S-97 thrilled her. Scott's eyes were closed tight as he sat rigid. They could hear Scooter being given directions to where Diego may be from back in the compound. The chopper sped above the main road that led out of the gate into the miles of citrus groves.

Within just a few minutes Scooter said, "I think I see the little bullbat up ahead." Scott opened his eyes. He saw a dust cone behind a boy speeding down a dirt road on what he thought might be a 125cc dirt bike.

"Aww, man. There's a yella jacket in the outhouse," Scooter said into his mic as he worked the chopper's controls to gain more speed.

Still learning all Scooter's Texas lingo, Mel didn't understand the yellow jacket in the outhouse reference until she saw a second dust cone behind Diego. With this she figured Scooter was saying something like Diego was in deep shit. Behind him was the pack of mutated dogs the guard tower had spied that morning. They were in pursuit of Diego and gaining on his six in a hurry.

Scooter punched a button, and the entire front windshield turned into an amazing heads-up display. Information was everywhere. There were a series of colored circles around Diego and the dogs. Scooter was trying to line up a shot with the S-97s .50-caliber minigun, but the dogs were too close behind the boy.

"Gol'damn, it's like baggin' flies. I cain't line up the shot without punchin' a hole or two in the kid," Scooter said, clearly frustrated.

At that moment Diego's motorcycle slid to one side. He overcorrected and nearly flew off the seat. To regain control of the dirt bike, Diego had to let off the throttle. This put the pack nearly on top of him.

"He's not going to make it!" Mel screamed, terrified to see the kid so close to death when all she could do was watch.

"Hold on!" Scooter yelled as the bottom seemed to fall out of the chopper as it rapidly dropped altitude.

Mel shrieked in surprise. Both Scott's legs flew up as he grabbed for anything to hold on to. It was like free-falling. Mel could feel herself hovering just above her seat, thankful she was buckled in. Quickly the chopper leveled out just a couple feet from the ground. Scooter pulled up alongside the pack and pressed a button that caused the door they'd entered to slide back.

"Scott!" Scooter yelled. "Put her in the shootin' harness."

It took Scott a second to understand, and then he unbuckled himself. Above the open door was a shoulder harness. He unsnapped its binding and pulled it down. It was connected by a thin cable to the top of the door frame. It was used to allow a soldier to lay down cover fire to suppress an enemy while soldiers entered or exited the chopper without fear of falling out. Following Scooter's instruction, Mel unbuckled and moved over to where Scott had the harness ready for her to slip her arms through. She did, and he clipped it tightly around her.

"Why am I doing this?" she yelled, confused. A panel raised up in the rear exposing several rifles.

"Give her the AR with the Red Dot Optics!" Scooter yelled back to them. "It's short, light, and easy to aim. She'll love it!" Mel wasn't sure she loved anything about this plan.

One of the dogs launched forward and nearly nipped Diego in his back. Diego was now scootched up on the bike's seat, nearly on the gas tank, screaming in terror.

"Brace yourself, Scott!" Scooter yelled. Then the chopper banked hard toward the pack of dogs, scattering them momentarily, buying Diego some much-needed distance from the pack, but it didn't last long. Scott was barely able to grab hold of one of what Scooter called the "oh shit handles" along the walls, keeping him from flying out the open door. Mel lost her footing, and her whole body swung out of the open door and dangled precariously in the air. One of the mutated beasts gnashed its huge jaws filled with rows of razor-sharp teeth at her just as she lifted her legs to swing herself back inside the door.

"Oh, you want some of this, you K9 freak!" Mel taunted.

The chopper leveled out, and Scott grabbed the AR and racked a bullet in the chamber, then handed it to Mel. She seemed to get the gist of what was expected of her now.

"What's the plan, Scooter?" Scott yelled with Mel now in the shooting harness, locked and loaded.

"We're gonna kill some rancid-breath demon dogs, that's what we're fixing to do, Scott!" Mel emphatically retorted, now intently focused out the door on her first target.

"Damn right!" he replied with a sideways grin. Seeing her all jacked up with the AR gripped tightly in her hands, seething with anger at those beasts, made him

94

flush for a second. Quickly getting his head back in the game, he turned to Scooter, who explained the plan.

"I'm gonna sidle up to the little booger, and you snatch his ass off that bike. Mel, you cover Scott with that rifle. Keep them unholy bitches from rippin' Scotty to bits," Scooter instructed, and sped up the chopper alongside Diego. As he paced the dirt bike's speed, he began to slowly guide the chopper closer to it. Diego looked over and nearly toppled himself, taking his attention off the road. Scott leaned out. The ground raced underneath him. Some of the taller scrub brush raked the underside of the chopper. Mel leaned out the door in the harness. She shouldered the compact rifle, put the red dot center mass of the closest mutant, and fired twice, causing it to buckle and roll away in the dust. Another eyed her angrily and started over toward her. They were so fast and agile that she almost wasn't able to twist and fire in time. The bullet just grazed its front flank enough to slow it down a beat. Then it was sprinting even faster, outrunning the others. Its muzzle was enlarged, and its lips twisted up garishly below two huge yellow eyes. Its long tongue flopped in and out of its mouth with each snap of its powerful jaws, sending spit and slobber in all directions. When it got just mere feet away from her, it powerfully leaped forward. She screamed and fired as its huge lion-like claws reached forward to shred her to bits. The bullet entered the beast's open mouth into the back of its throat. The back of its skull exploded into a huge spray of gore as it tumbled into the dust. Another had set its yellow eyes on her and sped forward now. She shot but just missed wide to its left, which seemed to piss it off even more, and it sped ahead of the pack. This got the attention of several others, which spurred another one in her direction. She didn't know which to shoot; they both were converging too fast.

The chopper closed in on Diego, and he glanced over. Seeing Scott's outreached arm, he tried to angle the dirt bike over without losing control.

"You better grab him now!" Scooter yelled, seeing ahead less than a hundred yards the concrete lip of a huge reservoir approaching.

"Jump!" Scott screamed at Diego. He, too, saw the reservoir ahead.

"Jump, dammit!" he yelled again. Diego looked over at Scott, then back ahead, shaking his head. Then he looked over at Scott again. For a split second Scott didn't think he was going to jump at all. He looked frozen with terror. Then he leapt toward Scott's arm, but his foot hooked the handlebars, diminishing his momentum as the dirt bike toppled and flipped out of control. He fell short of Scott's outreached hand, screaming. Mel was focused on the beast approaching from the right and was just about to squeeze off a short burst when she felt something grab her left leg. She panicked, thinking it was a beast biting her from the blind spot below the chopper. She swung the muzzle of the gun down, nearly shooting Diego in the head. He had wrapped his arms around her left leg and was being dragged across the dirt. A beast jumped at him as Mel fired into its chest, but the .223 round was no match for its powerful momentum. It continued forward onto Diego's legs. Its claws digging into his thigh. He screamed in agony. Mel dropped the rifle and reached down, grabbing one of his wrists just as he was torn away from her leg by the hooked claws. At that moment the chopper flew over the lip of the reservoir, and the beast holding Diego fell away with his jaws biting the air as it fell.

Scott reached down and hauled Diego onto the floor of the cabin as Scooter pulled back on the yoke, gaining altitude, then banked hard back toward the compound. Below, Mel could see several beasts from the vicious pack swimming around in the reservoir. A few others were able to stop shy of the concrete lip. They looked up at the retreating chopper full of hate, running in circles, jumping and biting the air.

Chapter Nine

Dr. Warwick Kerr sat at the head of a large conference room table at the Planet's Keepers headquarters in Isla de los Estados. Also crammed at the table and sitting along the walls were his most trusted disciples pledged to save Mother Earth. It wasn't often they all amassed in the same place. Each came from very diverse backgrounds and locations. They represented the global core of power for the Planet's Keepers. However, being physically together was the only way the second phase of Kerr's plan could work. They were reviewing the current state of what they called the animal apocalypse that would usher in the new Eden. The plan was going even better than his father could have ever imagined. It seemed the Chow brand of genetically weaponized pet food and supplements had permeated even the most remote corners of the globe. Kerr even heard stories of penguins in the Arctic circle mutating and slaughtering entire Eskimo villages. The thought of it made him chuckle.

No continent was immune, every country was becoming crippled, and no human would survive in the end. They weren't supposed to. Not even those in this room, unless they found safety. This was the challenge posed almost twenty years ago when Dr. Kerr started the planning for phase two: how to preserve the lives of the core disciples and their families. It was the escape plan to go somewhere out of reach of the mutated killing machines. Until the carnage of the mutations subsided and Mother Earth could restore itself to Eden, no human would be safe on this planet.

Dr. Kerr's father was initially only able to obtain the Chow company's recipes from that top secret folder in the chairman's office. Everything else he learned was from the brief peek he got at the rest of that file. Once he was back in his DC apartment, he wrote every single thing he recalled from that file into a new file of his own. He was puzzling out some things, but not nearly enough to bring the plan forward. It wasn't until he was able to buy the Chow company out of bankruptcy that he found many more critical details. He then had access to all of Chow's archived files. In 1972 there weren't computer backups into the cloud. Everything was on paper in handwritten labeled file boxes and stored in secure locations. He quickly located all the files he could and began pouring over them one page at a time. He was thrilled to learn the CIA had shut down the Supermoon Protocol so quickly. In their haste, they left behind many treasure troves of information, information never intended for eyes outside of a certain level of classification in the US government. Millions upon millions of dollars from Chow profits and private donations were poured into understanding the modified feed's genetic makeup and how it reacted to a certain gamma ray.

He essentially learned what the government scheme was: to transform the CIA's operation Organic Death into President Johnson's Supermoon Protocol to end the Vietnam War. It was simple, really. Drop genetically modified feed blocks that the jungle animals would be attracted to and consume. Then during the 1970 supermoon when the moon was at its closest distance to Earth, a custom-built gamma-ray device would trigger the mutant evolutions in the animals that had eaten the feed. The US military would then attack the Viet Cong from the outside of the jungles while the animal killing machines attacked them from within. The theory up to that point had actually been tested and proved successful. It was the next part of their plan that was hypothetical theory. They hoped that when the moon orbited back to its original distance from Earth, the evolutions would reverse, and thus the infected animals would either revert to their normal state or parish in short order due to the unsustainable biological makeup their newly evolved bodies would have. If that didn't happen, then their worst-case scenario was to napalm the hell out of the jungles in which the plan was applied, thus killing every last living creature.

Before the CIA could execute the plan, President Nixon canceled it. He had pretty much given up on President Johnson's vision of winning the Vietnam War and focused on just ending it, which he did in Paris in 1973 by signing the Paris Peace Accords. At this point the gamma-ray device had been installed and remained active on the moon. Retrieving it would be an enormous expense. They assumed it was benign just sitting there in the moon's normal orbit, out of range of the earth. And that was mostly correct. However, much more modified feed was consumed, and not just in a small jungle, but on a global scale. Dr. Kerr's father was able to turn the bankrupt pet food company into the world's most popular and widely purchased animal feed and supplement company in existence today. They were into more than pet foods now—everything from farm feed, exotic food used in zoos all over the globe, and animal feed nutritional supplements for domestic pets. Metric tons of Chow feed was consumed every day, and had been for the last fifty years, bringing the total infected animal population to over 130 billion, outnumbering the 7.8 billion humans by roughly 16 to 1.

"The human race is experiencing its demise. Complete eradication is practically guaranteed now. It can't be stopped," Dr. Kerr murmured with a smirk to the others in the room as he read the last of the infection reports. Several in the room voiced agreement, while others started applauding. Everyone wore a victorious grin. Dr. Warwick Kerr looked around the room allowing the accolades to wash over him. After a minute, he raised his hands to silence the exuberance.

Once the room was quieted, he said, "Phase two is a week off schedule. However, everyone should be safe here on the islands. A contingency for such a delay has been put into place. We've eradicated all animals that would be capable of infection prior to the supermoon and have seen no mutations since. Our heavily armed security team has a perimeter established and patrolling 24/7. These measures will only be effective in the short term, as our biggest vulnerabilities are via air and sea, which is why we must execute our evacuation plan as soon as the engineers give us the green light. The mutations will become more aggressive over the coming days as humans begin to thin out worldwide. For now, this is the safest place on Earth," he said with a smile, opening his arms wide. "Continue your endurance workouts and lunar training. You will need to be ready to load the transport pods at a moment's notice. I will convey any updates as they occur." He almost felt sorry for all the support staff making this feat possible. Only a select few would be joining the journey. All others assumed they would later be ferried by the pods once the first passengers were emptied on the moon. So goes life, he thought. There are always casualties in war, and this was the largest battlefront in human history.

With that, he stood and left the conference room and headed to the elevator. He scanned his key card and punched an unmarked button. The elevator went down nearly five hundred feet and opened to a long tubular hallway made of acrylic glass. On display outside the glass was pristine ocean life. Under the ocean's surface is still an Eden in its own way. It's above the sea where humans trample and defile the environment, killing Mother Earth. Dr. Kerr whistled the classic country tune by Travis Tritt, "It's a Great Day to be Alive," as he walked the length of the hallway that ended at a steel-reinforced door. This door was locked with a double biometric scanner. On one area he had to place his thumb to scan his print, and on the other he had to place his chin, which scanned his retinas. The heavy door hissed open revealing a cavernous room. Here several engineers were working around the clock putting the finishing touches on the transport pods the Planet's Keepers and their families would use to transport them to a location to wait out the animal apocalypse in safety. The passengers were given special luggage designed to survive this unique trip and maximize storage space in the confined pods. When they returned that glorious day in the future, they might find their worldly assets still intact. But even if all they owned were destroyed, what would it matter? The entire earth would be theirs to reinhabit and establish an eco-friendly civilization from the ground up. Everything and everyone would serve Mother Earth in the new Eden. A utopian paradise.

The pods relied on driverless technology, which was the reason for the current delay. A software glitch. The latest dry run was almost a success. The test pod failed to dock appropriately, missing its mark by just mere fractions of an inch. This caused a gap in the air lock, which would have killed all the passengers within seconds. Fractions of an inch doesn't sound like a big deal, except it is—a really big deal since the pods would be docking in space where precision is a matter of life and death. When Dr. Kerr began planning for this second phase, he understood finding pilots to fly these pods would be virtually impossible within his discipleship. Technology would serve as the ship's captains, and Dr. Kerr saw this technological answer in the emerging efforts of driverless car technology.

Truly autonomous cars appeared in the 1980s, with Carnegie Mellon University's Navlab and ALV projects in 1984 and Mercedes-Benz and Bundeswehr University Munich's Eureka Prometheus Project in 1987. Decades later Google had taken the largest steps in the driverless arena and turned their project into a company called Waymo. Funding to pursue this technology in the US was dominated by Waymo, which topped out at $5.5 billion by the Alphabet company, and by the Cruise company, which was backed with $10 billion from GM, Honda, and other investors, in addition to a $5 billion line of credit from GM Financial.

Ultimately, through the years, the talent pool in this industry expanded greatly. So did the concept of environmentalism. This made it easier to recruit such intelligent minds into his fold. To serve something greater, like Mother Earth, it took a person who was on a higher intelligence plane, and today's top universities were pumping out these enlightened students in droves. Dr. Kerr was a master motivator and team builder. He had finally amassed a diverse engineering team that proved extremely capable in advancing driverless technology. Applying driverless capabilities from terrestrial vehicles to those that traverse air and space was an exciting challenge for this team. Now they were within a matter of days of perfecting what the industry had been struggling with for years, the AI component. The Black Box of virtual intelligence needed to fly through unpredictable circumstances. In space, the unpredictable unknown loomed large and exciting.

Dr. Kerr was seen but not heard as he casually strolled around the cavernous workspace. He understood the concept of empowerment and despised micromanagement. He'd learned this from his father too.

"Set clear, bold expectations, then turn the talent loose to do what they do best, all the while compensating and praising individual and team achievements," his father told his young son, Warwick. He often explained that his role was to support the teams in this way.

And the results had been fabulous. As Dr. Kerr stood there watching the individual teams focused on their specific tasks, he brimmed with excitement and had full confidence the software glitch would be resolved in very short order. He often found himself wishing his father was here to see this, but he knew his father's spirit was alive and well within the Planet's Keepers.

The flight from Reynosa, Mexico, to Washington, DC, was set for just under three hours. In a plush leather reclining seat in the rear of the plane, resting his eyes, sat Benjamin Masters. The events of the last few days weighed heavy on him now that he had nothing better to do than just sit there in his seat. He hoped to catch a much-needed nap, but his mind couldn't stop churning through thoughts of the past and this upcoming meeting with Trey Lett. The fact Lett reached out to him directly spoke to the seriousness of this meeting, and Masters was thinking hard to predict Lett's reasoning for it.

Masters figured he must have learned the truth about what happened in Chetumal back in 1999, the truth about his daughter. She and Masters had just come off a political assignment in Venezuela when the CIA was approached by the DEA about a drug cartel investigation they were working on that stemmed from Columbia. The Columbians were moving raw cocaine up the coast and handing it off to the Mexicans, who in turn processed it and distributed it in America. The DEA needed to know where the handoff point to the Mexicans was. They figured the fastest way to learn would be to embed someone into the cartel's workflow to discover it. The DEA knew from time to time the Columbian cartel would hire local fishermen in that area to transport the drugs.

The DEA resources were stretched thin already, and the assets they had stationed in the area were already too well known. So they asked the CIA, who also operated in that area, if they had someone to loan the DEA for this single assignment. Since Masters and Lett's daughter were already there and had some bandwidth, they were assigned to the DEA to pose as a husband-and-wife fishing outfit. They set them up with a fishing boat and all the authentic resources they would need to create the facade of fishing the area the DEA figured the drugs were being transported through. Sure enough, after six months, their boat was hailed and boarded by the Colombians. They searched the fishing vessel and then made a proposition to Masters to smuggle a shipment of cocaine to a small village called Chetumal up the Mexican coast. Like the locals, they played the part of needing the money and an eagerness to please the true power in the region. Declining these propositions from the cartel meant death, and the locals knew it.

It wasn't until the delivery in Chetumal was complete that things took a turn for the worse. Masters and Lett's daughter walked away from the assignment, successfully able to expose the handoff point to the DEA. 'Twas the night before their extraction was scheduled, in a small beach bar on New Year's Eve that they were kidnapped by the Mexican cartel and transported to an undisclosed location where they were tortured. Trey Lett's daughter didn't survive, and Masters was beyond lucky to have escaped. When Masters resurfaced, the questions about Lett's daughter were answered. However, the DEA was waging a political battle for their own agency's survival on Capitol Hill. The war on drugs was lost, and our government knew it. Uncountable amounts of money had gone into waging it, and many leaders were ready to pull the plug, and Trey Lett had the power to do it as the then-Senate majority leader. It was decided by the higher-ups in the DEA to lie to Lett. They led him to believe his daughter was still alive and being held prisoner. They figured if he thought this was true, he would be less eager to wind down the DEA in that area in hopes they would ultimately rescue her. This ruse went on for many years after. Now that Lett had the keys to all the intelligence agencies as the National Security Director, Masters figured he now knew the truth about his daughter and, worse, the gruesome fashion in which she died.

Masters suddenly felt ill recalling the devastation he felt when he learned that the CIA was going along with the DEA's farce of a story. At the time he was 100 percent devoted to the agency. He had served it well, and they always had his back both operationally and personally. He knew this decision to lie to Trey Lett about his daughter's death was political and further up the food chain than Masters's own superiors. He was glad to learn he wasn't the only one in his ranks disturbed by this decision. Over time this caused a rift in one of the few government agencies that rarely feuded internally. Soon a group devoted to the agency's integrity wanted to clear the air and come clean about what had happened to Senator Lett's daughter. The opposition group felt if the truth ever was exposed, then the agency's credibility on many clandestine operations would also start to be picked apart in a slippery slope turned witch hunt.

Then Masters started having debilitating nightmares. At first there were sleep disturbances here and there. Then a theme developed and compounded until it became all-consuming, robbing him of any meaningful sleep. He started to act erratically but was able to hold it together, until on one mission he completely botched a pickup of a secret asset in the Middle East that nearly got them both killed and risked exposing the whole operation. Masters was reprimanded and required to see a shrink, but by this time he was becoming truly unpredictable. The agency bureaucrats began to view him as a liability for keeping his prior partner's death under wraps. They failed on a haphazardly coordinated hit on him upon his return to the US, putting Masters on the run and labeled a fugitive within the CIA.

Thankfully, during his years with the agency, Masters had forged many trusted relationships among his peers. These trusted friends helped him stay one step ahead of the agency's efforts to bring him in. Through these contacts he learned Rob Florchett was having similar nightmares and the agency was after him, too, in fear he would expose a separate cover-up of the CIA— one of a certain night in North Dallas in 1970 that sent

Rob's grandfather to prison for the attempted murder of his family. If Rob's insomniac condition was traced back to that night, it would expose the reckless handling of decommissioning President Johnson's Supermoon Protocol assets, which included the Chow company and their secret weaponized GMO feed recipe. It was later suspected the GMO feed formula may have gotten out, but no initiative was taken to tie up that loose end. No agency wanted responsibility or wanted to take the blame for the implications. Masters knew the return of his sanity hung in the balance of finding Rob Florchett, which he did, and thankfully. That led to Dr. Sheltie, who had the means to cure them both. That was just three days ago, yet it seemed much longer given all the events packed into the few days since.

So this meeting with Trey Lett could only be because he had found out about his daughter's death. Either Masters was about to be scapegoated and arrested, or Lett genuinely wanted to give Masters a chance to tell his side of the story. He hoped for the latter because it would be the only way Lett would ever learn of the real truth, as ugly and disturbing as it was.

****

"No! We have to go back! They need help!" Diego pleaded through his tears as Scott tied his belt as a tourniquet around the boy's gushing thigh.

"You're losing too much blood, kid," Scott explained, packing the nastiest gash with gauze Mel passed him from a first aid kit and then wrapping it all with a bandage.

"I don't care! She called me this morning saying that an entire herd of cattle is destroying their village. Please!"

Scott looked up at Mel, and their eyes met briefly. He could see in them concern for the boy's girlfriend and village. It was a new look from her usual "I gotta chip on my shoulder."

Scott yelled into the comm, "Scooter? Did you hear what the boy said?"

"Yep."

"What do you think?"

"You got his wounds licked good?"

"Yeah, his bleeding seems under control, but he's lost a lot."

"Think he'll make it another half hour or so?"

"Yeah, that shouldn't be a problem."

"Then I say we go charbroil some beef!" Scooter exclaimed. "Show y'all what Texas BBQ is all about!"

And with that the chopper veered hard to the right back toward the village. The S-97 raced across the sky. Scott and Mel kept working on Diego's wounds until he was as good as he was gonna get with what they had in the way of first aid. Mel watched Scott work on the wounds. His hands were gentle with the severe lacerations. He was good with Diego, even made him laugh a few times, diverting his attention when Scott knew it was gonna hurt to touch. Was that charming? She shrugged off the thought and looked out the front windshield just as Scooter announced they were approaching the outskirts of the village.

"Wooo, doggies," Scooter said, amazed at the evolved cattle coming into view. Several were grouped together over the bodies of villagers.

"Are those bodies?" Mel gasped.

Diego bolted upright, hearing Mel, anxious to see if it was Ariana or her family. On the windscreen's HUD, a circle around the group of cattle went from green to red.

"Yep. Good thing they're already dead though. They won't be feelin' this," Just as he said that, an AGM-114 Hellfire missile jumped into view, streaking into the center of the mutant cattle. A huge explosion bloomed, incinerating most of the beasts into a splattering of flames.

"Ha ha ha ha, how you city slickers like your ribeyes?" Scooter yelled energetically into his rearview mirror at Mel and Scott, clearly enjoying himself. Mel had to admit what she had just seen was pretty freaking cool.

"Maybe y'all are in the mood for some smoked brisket?" he yelled. "Coming right up!" Then he released another Hellfire missile into another large group of cattle, sending flaming chunks of meat in all directions. Several beasts now scattered. Scooter gave chase as the HUD system locked onto each target. This was the ultimate thrill ride experience. Mel didn't understand how the .50-caliber autocannon worked, but each target was obliterated one after the other in amazing sprays of blood and flesh. Everyone, including Diego, was whooping and hollering in the chopper as Scooter laid waste to the evolutionary abominations. The graceful yet amazingly powerful chopper was exhilarating, weaving hairpin turns. It was just like a video game through the front windscreen. Even on the ground, several villagers were peeking out for a look and cheering Scooter on. He was having the time of his life as he realized he'd killed all the demon heifers.

"Aww hell, I was just beginning to enjoy myself," Scooter said, truly disappointed. He swung the helicopter around to head back to the compound when something caught Diego's eye.

"Wait! Look over there!"

Everyone turned and looked where Diego was pointing. A collective groan filled the comm units.

"Oh sheeit! That's one huge motha humpa right there," Scooter breathed. Standing in the middle of the central courtyard was the biggest bull any of them had ever seen, even Scooter, who had seen plenty back home in Texas. It had a large group of villagers cornered. Scattered around the bull were several slashed-apart bodies of those that had tried to escape. The bull was snorting and pawing the ground, toying with them.

"That there is a Charbray bull straight from the depths of rodeo hell that'll turn any cowboy into a jump chump," Scooter explained, astonished.

"How can you tell?" Scott asked. The mutant was massive and hardly resembled any bull he'd ever seen. It had to weigh over ten thousand pounds of solid, rippling muscle. Its rear flanks were as wide as a Buick. On its head were four huge horns that curved forward into needle points. It had huge golden eyes set above massive tusks extruding from under its slimy jowls. It paced side to side with amazing agility for its size.

"They're a crossbreed with a Brahma bull and Satan himself. They have that orange-colored fur and a huge dewlap hangin' from their necks. The meanest of the mean and baddest of the bad in the rodeo world," Scooter answered.

While he was educating Scott on the bull's lineage, he began slowly easing the chopper closer to it, hoping to get its attention from the cornered throng of people.

Suddenly, the bull turned his head up at the encroaching object in the sky. It turned and raised up on its hind legs and let out a loud bellowing roar, biting the air with its huge tusks. Two men in the group took advantage of the bull's attention being diverted and took off running. This drew its attention back to the group, and like a shot, it ran them down, goring both on its horns like shish kebabs. Its strong neck lowered, and then it slung its head back, sending the men's bodies sailing up to the roof of a nearby building. Their entrails rained down on the ground in huge splats.

Panicked, a young boy broke free from his mom's grip as she held a baby in her other arm. She screamed for him to stop, then ran after him, but it was too late. The bull charged the kid with amazing speed and grabbed him in its powerful jaws, crunching his body and then slinging it aside into a broken heap with the others. The bull now focused its hatred on the exposed woman holding the baby. She froze where she stood in complete terror.

"Scooter, shoot it!" yelled Mel.

Scooter was fighting the weapons console in the HUD. Colored circles were dancing everywhere.

"I can't! Those people are too close. We need to draw the bull out of the city center where I can get a shot off at it."

The bull began pawing the ground, preparing to charge the woman.

"Hey, you nasty bastard! Look up here, you deranged son of a bitch!" Scooter was screaming, then whistling into the chopper's PA system. The bull looked up, annoyed at the sound, but then refocused its attention on the woman.

"Lower me down!" Scott demanded. Mel glanced at him quickly with mixed emotions at his bravado.

"I'll distract him out into the open."

"Hower you gonna do that?" Scooter asked.

"I don't know, but I can't sit here and watch the death of those innocent people." Scooter hesitated to lower the chopper to the ground after he saw how quickly the mutant bull was. He didn't think he could lift the chopper quick enough if it charged. Instead, he flipped an overhead switch, and a panel in the floor slid open, exposing a chain ladder on an electric winch that started to lower down. Scott took off his comm unit and quickly began climbing through the hole, down the ladder.

"Scott, wait! Don't, please!" Mel found herself pleading, but he was down too far, and without his comm unit on, he couldn't hear her over the rumble of the chopper.

Scott skipped the last four rungs and jumped down. The bull turned and took notice. It looked back at the woman, then back at Scott, then chose the moving challenge versus the sitting duck. It galloped toward Scott, its eyes blazing with hate. He hadn't assessed the best direction to lead the bull, so he opted to go opposite the throng of villagers. The earth shook violently as the bull hit its stride. Scott risked a look back, and the bull was merely twenty feet behind him. He had reached the edge of a circular fountain marking the center of the courtyard. In the middle of it stood a thirty-foot concrete statue of some Mexican village founder with its arm outstretched, pointing to the future or, more likely, the way Scott should have run. Scott jumped up and pushed off the edge of the fountain and flung himself onto the statue, landing just above its waist. He shimmied up quickly and wrapped himself around the figure's head.

The bull was running at top speed, its huge hooves thundering like a single steer stampede. Without slowing, it, too, reached up the side of the fountain wall with its front legs, then pushed off with its hind legs, soaring into the air. It lowered its head to gore Scott. Scott swung his legs up as high as he could, gripping the statue's forehead. The bull centered the crown of its head into the statue's chest, its deadly horns just shy of Scott's back. The statue exploded into chalky dust and crushed concrete. Still clinging to the statue's head, Scott fell into the fountain with a huge splash. The bull writhed around in midair realizing had it missed its mark, and landed hard on its side, then rolled several times and skidded to a halt.

Scott surfaced out of the water gasping for air, rubbing the water out of his face trying to get eyes on the bull. He saw the bull try to stand and then stumbled, clearly dazed. Its skull poured bright crimson from cramming against the statue. It shook its head wildly, slinging blood and drooling everywhere. Scott took this chance to stand and motion all the villagers out of the courtyard. The group didn't hesitate as several men herded the women and children along to safety. The bull unsteadily gained its feet. It narrowed its glowing eyes on Scott and reared back on its hind legs bellowing a hideous yell, then raced at Scott with its head lowered for the kill.

Scott heard the bellow and saw the bull charging. He now had an idea of the direction he should run, but the mutant was so very fast. He wasn't going to make it and saw a truck parked to his right and ran for it. The bull

kept an unwavering bead on its target, never slowing.
Scott jumped into the bed of the truck and scrambled
onto its roof just as the beast smashed into the truck's
side, sending Scott straight up in the air and the truck
flipping over like a toy. He landed square on the bull's
back. Lying flat, he couldn't get a grip on the beast. The
skin was slick with sweat and rippling with sinewy
muscles flexing beneath it. The bull started to buck,
kicking up its huge flanks, causing Scott to flip around.
Scott slid down toward the beast's head. His shoes found
the backs of the bull's horns as it reared its head back.
Scott used the upward momentum and jumped as hard as
he could, catapulting himself dozens of feet into the air
and landing hard on his back. All the wind was brutally
knocked out of him as he rolled over struggling to
breathe.

The bull turned angrily in circles searching for
Scott. It finally located him as he raised up onto one knee.
It lowered its head to deliver the killing blow. Scott knew
he was toast. No way he was going to escape this. He
contemplated the best way, as if there was one, to get
gored to death. Just when he decided standing sideways

might be the best, he heard someone whistle and yell from behind the bull.

"Hey! You sorry sack of cow shit!"

The bull turned at the intruder. It was Mel. She was waving her arms in big circles, trying to get the bull's attention off of Scott. It seemed to work as the bull slowly turned toward Mel, then looked back at Scott, who now was standing unsteadily to his feet. The bull was fixed between them both, seemingly trying to decide which target it should pursue. It chose Mel. Then Scott began waving his arms and yelling. The bull paused, looking back at Scott vying for its attention. Finally, it let out a huge huff of demonic breath, raising a cloud of dust around it, and turned back and charged Mel.

"No! NO!" Scott yelled. He panicked, breaking into a sprint after it.

Meanwhile Scooter was circling the S-97 around, putting it in position to fire at the broadside of the bull as it charged Mel. At least that was their plan. With Scott in pursuit, it made Scooter's shot much more difficult. Also, Mel didn't factor in the sheer terror of being chased by such an abomination, and she veered off course, running directly toward the chopper instead of perpendicular to it.

"Aww heck. She's as confused as a goat on Astroturf," muttered Scooter, quickly assessing his options. Then a thought occurred to him. Mounted in a flush canister in the nose of the chopper was a new weapon from DARPA. They call it a stun light. It was a super-concentrated beam of light that was fifty times more intense than an aircraft landing light. Just a small burst could be fatally debilitating and totally incapacitating to any living thing. Scooter wondered if the mutant bull was in the category of living. He flipped the toggle on his yoke, causing the HUD to activate and aim the stun light. The beam of light could be narrowed with precision, so he tried to focus it on the front of the bull, saving Mel and Scott from being blasted too.

Mel tripped and rolled onto her back. She sat up, and the bull was coming too fast for her to move. She balled herself up, preparing for the horns. She felt a rush of intense heat flash her body. Then she felt the earth begin quaking. Just ten feet from her, the bull was skidding on its side, bucking and flopping toward her. She quickly got to her feet and dove out of the way before it crashed down where she had been sitting. Scott diverted his course and followed Mel, running away from the bull, leaving it in the wide open space just outside the village. Scooter switched off the stun light. The bull was now standing but totally blind. It swung its head this way and that, making a horrendous grunting noise. Blood poured from where its eyes once were, and a river of saliva flowed off its lolling tongue and slung off its jowls as it searched frantically for its prey.

"Time to send ye back to the hell from which thy came," Scooter cooed gently just as the HUD's green circle around the bull turned bright red and a Hellfire missile found its way directly up the mutant bull's Buick-sized ass.

Chapter Ten

The room wasn't small, but it wasn't large either. No overhead lights were on. There were about a dozen cubicles clustered together in its center. Each contained its own lighting preference. Some were just lit by computer screens, and others had strings of Christmas lights. It smelled of ozone, electricity, and stale food. In a corner was a four-post server rack containing all sorts of computer networking equipment with hundreds of rapidly blinking green and orange LEDs. The hundreds of servers themselves were housed in a fully self-sustained and redundant tier 4–rated data center below this room. The sound of software programmers clattering away at their keyboards was like a lullaby to his ears as he stood in the doorway of his office looking out into the darkened Pit, as it was called. Located thirteen stories under the ocean, the Pit was home to some of the most talented software developers and hackers in the entire world. And the man leaning against the doorframe looking on was their leader, Rodnell Cook.

Cook was not a programmer, but rather a very talented aerospace engineer that had focused most of his career on lunar travel. He was recruited by his then girlfriend into the Planet's Keepers during his junior year at the University of Glasgow, the UK's premiere aerospace engineering school. He was never serious about the activism they engaged in, but more interested in scoring points with the girl that would later become his wife. His dream was to join the Royal Navy to obtain his flight training. Then after a few years work toward making Britain a global player in space exploration. Since he was a child, he dreamt of leading a British space expedition to the moon, even Mars or beyond.

During his last year in the Royal Navy, he received word of a terrorist attack in a London shopping mall. A bomb was activated in the crowded food court, sending hundreds of ball bearings in all directions, killing dozens and injuring more. Amongst the casualties were his new wife and their infant son. She was breastfeeding him on an out-of-the-way bench. A single steel bearing from the blast went through both his son's and his wife's hearts. They died instantly. Cook was devastated. Unable to focus on much any longer, he was honorably discharged from the navy. The British authorities caught the terrorists responsible, but to the public's chagrin, he learned the Crown wasn't pressing charges against the bastards because of a social experiment by the government to lessen aggression toward domestic Muslims in hopes of easing heightening tensions. He and other angry families railed against the justice system, only to be placated and told their sacrifice was for the greater good. Cook became enraged. How dare they put his family's lives below those of terrorist scum. He retaliated by beating the politician sponsoring the government's experiment within an inch of his life. Cook spent four years in prison. He lost his faith in his government and mankind in general. Finally, he was up for parole and was told there was no chance he would get it. The politician he beat up was seeing to it.

During his parole hearing, someone present was influential in UK politics, Dr. Warwick Kerr. The Planet's Keepers had deep influence on many governments across the globe from donating billions to curry favor when needed. And Kerr needed Cook's aerospace expertise. Kerr's father had taught him to seek out the most vulnerable yet talented people and save them from their plight, and if successful, they'd never have to worry about their loyalty. Kerr spoke on Cook's behalf at the hearing, explaining that Cook's anger was misguided and he himself would be willing to work with Cook on focusing his energy into a noble cause—saving the planet. The liberal judge presiding over the hearing allowed for it, due in small part to a generous campaign donation by the Planet's Keepers, of course. Cook was released on probation into Dr. Kerr's custody.

Cook was very grateful, but curious why this man had gone through such an effort to free him. The Planet's Keepers wasn't where Cook held his loyalty. He really couldn't give a fig about the planet. It was the revelation of Kerr's plan to populate the dark side of the moon that Rodnell gave his full loyalty to. The plan was ballsy and beyond clever. It would be the challenge he was born for, and growing up as a black kid in a European country, he knew he would never get this chance again. Building out the vehicles and infrastructure of the moon colony had him beyond excited. He knew a man like Dr. Kerr had the means and will to do it, and if humankind would be annihilated along with the UK and all the social experimental bullshit, all the better. Now justice was being served, and Rodnell was a huge part of ushering it in.

"I found the issue!" yelled an awkward pubescent voice from inside the darkened cubicle farm. Cook knew that crackly voice. It was one of the recent kid prodigies he'd discovered by trolling hacking chat rooms on the dark web. This was where Cook did most of his recruiting. Cook's chat handle was Dark Moon. He would look for specific personalities and those who were working on cracking code that many would think utterly impossible. It was those hackers who were bored with the chore of stealing identities and making money. That was too easy. They were hacking for the challenge, the respect toward higher street credit amongst their peers. For the love of it. He found this kid and seduced him into working on small programs designed by Cook's team, which he used as a training course of sorts, to vet newbies. The kid passed easily and actually turned some of the code against itself, thus crashing their system. Cook had to have him.

While the kid was running Cook's proving ground gauntlet, Cook was looking into the kid's background. Into his family life. Into his finances and affiliations. Everything looked perfect. A loner, orphaned, and no familial ties. He had a single bank account of nearly $2 million. Charges to the account were mostly to technology stores, with the occasional subscription fees to various online services and sites. Once the decision was made to bring him onto the team, Cook staked out the kid's house. The boy never left it, but his foster parents often did. After eavesdropping on the mother's cell, Cook learned that she and her husband would be out overnight. This was when Cook made his move, and with a team of two, broke into the kid's house. As Cook imagined, when he opened the door to the kid's room, it was dark save for the glow of three huge LCD displays and the silhouette of a twelve-year-old boy's bulbous head in the center.

It didn't take much persuading to bring the kid into the fold. They stole away that night to a private jet that brought them to the Pit, the boy's new home. His name was Percy, but everyone called him Kid. He was a decade younger than anyone else on the team. Like most of the others in his ranks, he was a misfit and quickly settled in. It impressed Cook just how fast the youngster caught up to speed. Cook knew deep down it would be the kid that would find and fix the issue. He was that amazing. Cook made his way over to the kid's cubicle and looked over his shoulder as the boy's fingers blurred on his backlit gamer's keyboard.

"What do you got?" Cook said in his deep voice. Kid may have been a kid, but Cook treated him as an adult.

"The problem was in one of the simple Boolean calculations that assisted in the docking computation. The AI split the difference in the logic, leaving the vessel to dock short, creating the air gap."

"What do you mean there *was* a problem?"

"I fixed it. Now watch the simulator code," Kid said as he tapped the Enter key to run the freshly compiled code. A small group had formed behind Kid. Cook knew just enough about what he was seeing to grasp that the issue appeared to be resolved. There were grunts and murmurs from the others that indicated the depth of the boy's genius in how he fixed the issue.

When the simulator program finished, Cook said, "Get this loaded into Solomon for a dry run. Let me know when it's ready." Cook didn't offer any verbal praise to Kid, only gave him a subtle shoulder squeeze. Kid knew he did good and looked up at Cook like a proud son to this father.

Solomon was the transport craft's physical simulator replica. It took its name from King Solomon, who built the first temple in Jerusalem that ushered in a new era in the Christian religion, just as this Solomon would do for the religion of Mother Earth. It stood atop several hydraulic legs that moved in almost the identical sequences the actual craft would experience on its journey to the moon. Beside it was the lunar docking port that the craft had to marry against with exact precision. Success in the simulated environment would give Cook the confidence needed before an actual flight was undertaken. The transport pods were just too expensive to test in reality, not to mention the travel time.

Cook sat at his desk after sending the email update to Dr. Kerr. His response was, "Excellent work. Now when precisely will we be ready to start loading the pods for launch?"

It did irk him a little that Kerr was rushing him and not allowing an actual test run to be performed. It needed to be tested on a dry run. If today's Solomon simulation test succeeded, he would go to Kerr and implore him to allow a dry run to be completed. The lives aboard were not just any people. They were the biggest in each business sector, and their wealth made up a third of all private wealth in the world. They would need these people and their money when the Planet's Keepers returned to the new Eden. But more importantly to Cook, his reputation was on the line. No, his life was on the line. This unforeseen delay was unacceptable to Kerr, and Cook could feel the tension growing between them. If the transport failed and all aboard were killed, Cook knew he would endure the same fate. Kerr would kill him, no doubt about it.

****

The Gulfstream touched down at Reagan International Airport. The jolt awoke Masters, who had finally dozed. He wiped his eyes and stretched. He looked further into the plane's cabin and saw that both Dr.

Sheltie and Rob had fallen asleep too. They stretched and worked to shake off their deep slumber. Everyone was so exhausted, he was glad they were able to catch a much-needed nap. The plane rolled to a stop, and the door was open almost immediately. As Masters stood to gather his things, a sharp-dressed woman entered the plane and strode directly to him. He figured she was an aide of some sort. Probably Lett's.

"Hello, Agent Masters," she said.

"I'm a former agent now," he replied with a grunt as he stood and stretched his long limbs. She continued without acknowledging his comment.

"A car is waiting outside to take you and your colleagues to Director Lett's office. Security is high due to the circumstances with the animals, so you will be surrounded at all times by a contingent of marines. Director Lett asked me personally to assure you this is for that reason and none other. You are not being detained; it is for your safety."

"I understand," Masters replied, although not entirely trusting.

"If you all will follow me," she indicated as she turned and walked back toward the door.

"What do you think?" Dr. Sheltie asked Masters as he walked by her and Rob. She could see his features were dour and severe. Nowhere was the usual air of confidence and superiority he usually exuded. She thought he might actually look frightened.

"I think we have no choice," he answered, and strode out the door.

"I'm not liking the way this feels," Dr. Sheltie said to Rob as she followed behind Masters.

"Me either," answered Rob behind her.

A cool, humid wind buffeted Rob as he emerged from the jet's door. The strong presence of jet fuel and smoke awoke any senses still lagging from his slumber. He followed Dr. Sheltie down the jet bridge, taking in the sight of several marines gathered in a circle with their backs around a black Suburban. To his right across the runway were several large passenger jets askew, some cocked on their sides, a few awash in huge jet fuel–fed flames. There were no emergency personnel, no fire brigade. No one. Anywhere.

The soldiers parted as Masters approached and one opened his door. Dr. Sheltie slid in next, followed by Rob. The door slammed shut and the armored beast roared forward. Behind them, Rob watched the soldiers load into jeeps and followed suit. They zipped between hangars and then through a gate that led out of the airport. He figured there once were guards there. Now there were none to be seen, and the heavy gates lay wide open. They raced through the streets of DC. Cars and trucks were abandoned, wrecked, some burning. Buildings were aflame. Many were ashen husks, still smoking. Not any sign of people anywhere. It was very eerie and quiet.

No one spoke in the Suburban either. The sharp-dressed lady who might have been an aide was silent, too, but had her mirror visor down, watching their every move. They took Interstate 66 across the Potomac River and exited onto Constitution Avenue, weaving in and out of discarded and abandoned vehicles. They raced by the Washington Monument, then the Smithsonian. Not a single person in view. It was like humans had vanished into thin air. Rob recalled when he was a small child in Sunday school learning about the rapture in which Jesus would come back for the saved. He always imagined this was what it would look like to a degree, but there would still be all the unsaved huddled in masses scared for their own salvation. But there were none, not a single one.

They turned onto Northwest Drive, entering the Capitol's grounds. Even here there were no people. No protestors, no guards fending them off. Just the roar of the huge V-8 in the eerie silence.

"We are approaching the garage entrance now," said the driver on his radio.

"Copy that. Enter quickly. Over," came the crackled response.

They drove down into a concrete driveway leading underground toward a large gate. Suddenly, the driver locked up the brakes, pressing everyone in the Suburban into their set belts. The fortified gate ahead started to open.

"Don't open the gate! Repeat, do not open the gate!" the driver yelled into the radio. A massive black gorilla had jumped down in front of them from the top of the driveway. It stood at least eight feet tall and had massive arms. Its eyes were huge with that yellow glow, and it bared its huge flesh-tearing teeth. It turned to the Suburban standing tall, pushing out its huge chest. It roared loudly and began beating it, making deep, sickening thwacks that could be felt inside the Suburban.

It sprinted quickly toward the truck and jumped high into the air, landing and crushing the hood, killing the engine instantly. It reared back its fist and slammed it into the bulletproof windscreen. The glass spiderwebbed in all directions and caved into the vehicle. The sharp-dressed aide-looking woman screamed, trying to unbuckle herself. The driver pulled out his service piece as the gorilla roared even louder and pushed through the glass, grabbing him by his face with its huge hand. Several errant shots went off from the driver's gun, one into the chest of the sharp-dressed aide as she scrambled between the seats trying to get into the back. She collapsed between Masters and Dr. Sheltie, blood streaming from her mouth as she sucked in wet breaths for help.

"Everyone get down!" Masters yelled. He knew what was coming next as the gorilla crushed the driver's head and yanked it free of the man's neck. Rob was in the very back row, literally crawling under the seat. Dr. Sheltie dove over the middle row, then nearly on top of Rob. Gunfire erupted from every direction outside the vehicle as the gorilla clawed its way through the front window. It screamed its baritone roar. It grabbed the back of the passenger seat, ripping it forward into the dash. Masters reared his legs back and gave the beast a sharp kick in its distorted face. The beast's head snapped back as it reached for Masters's legs. Fully enraged it crawled into the front cab, but struggled as its girth wedged it. It pressed its back up, and the roof creased up, slowly opening the front window space a bit more.

Masters rolled to his right toward the passenger side of the bench and tried to open the doors. They were jammed. The beast had bent the roof in a way that had the tops of the doors jammed tight. More bullets erupted, smacking into the sides of the vehicle. Loud smacks with bits of glass sprinkled in from bullets cracking into the bulletproof glass. He lunged into the back row as the beast grabbed his ankle. It was nearly all the way in the cab now. Masters twisted and with his other leg gave the animal a hard heel to its nose, crushing it. It let go of his leg and yelled furiously, sending a spray of its blood everywhere. Masters reached over the rear seat and was able to open the rear doors. He tumbled out, then stood and grabbed Rob's arm and pulled him out from under the seat. Once Rob was clear out on the concrete, he reached back for Dr. Sheltie. The abomination was completely inside the cab now and hurled its bulk over the middle row, arms grabbing for Masters. Its body was wedged again between the top of the last row and the roof. Dr. Sheltie was under the seat, hands clamped over her mouth trying to contain her panic. Two soldiers came around and unloaded a barrage of bullets into the beast's face and upper body. It bucked up hard into the roof, over and over until the roof split like a soda can and it tried to claw its way out. With its head and arms now out of the top of the Suburban, the two soldiers emptied their magazines into the beast's midsection, practically shredding it in two. The huge ape fell forward over the rear roof, and its huge arms dangled over the rear opening, making the Suburban nearly pop a wheelie. Everyone paused in the silence, watching and waiting.

Masters slowly approached one of the arms and gave it a push. It swung freely. He slowly reached through the cascade of blood that started pouring down the back. He took Dr. Sheltie's wrists, dragging her out from under the rear seat through the bloody waterfall and into his arms. She was shaken up pretty badly.

"Oh, Ben!" she sobbed into his neck.

"It's OK, you're safe now. It's dead," he replied, holding her tight. Rob watched as his head began to clear. He never took Masters as one to comfort anyone, but he was taking extra care to make sure Dr. Sheltie was alright.

"Sir, we need to get inside," a soldier came up and said. He was breathing heavily and clearly nervous as he pulled at Masters and motioned for Rob to get up and get moving. They were led through the gate into an underground parking garage as the heavy gate closed behind them.

"I'll take you where you can clean up. Director Lett is keen on seeing each of you as soon as possible," the soldier explained as they rode up the elevator. The doors opened, and two women who appeared to be custodians helped Dr. Sheltie into a women's washroom. Masters went into the men's, leaving Rob waiting for them both in the hallway. The guard moved down the hall speaking on a cell phone. Rob overheard the guard talking about many mutated animals that escaped from the Smithsonian National Zoo, which was literally next door. That explained the gorilla attack. After several minutes, Masters emerged from the men's room.

"You OK, Master Rob?" he asked, seemingly back in his usual character.

"Yeah, that was crazy. I hope Dr. Sheltie is OK."

"She is a very strong woman. She'll be fine, you'll see," he said, then turned to the guard for further instructions.

Chapter Eleven

They were in the Rurales infirmary. It was brightly lit and smelled of cleaning chemicals. Scooter, Scott, and the Rurales captain worked on everyone's wounds.

"I am sorry for being short-handed. We usually have the infirmary manned by two nurses at any given time. However, even they have taken leave to be with their families," said the captain, doing his best to stitch up a small shoulder wound on Scott.

Scott, in turn, was working on stitching and dressing Diego's more serious leg lacerations since he had the most medical training of the group. Scooter worked on some superficial scratches on Mel's legs and arms. While they worked, they explained the events of the last few hours to the captain. He held a stern face, his brow furrowed, looking at his nephew.

"It's not Diego's fault. He wanted to help Ariana and her village," Mel explained, trying to bring the captain's temperature down. She could see he was extremely agitated with Diego.

"I admire his bravado, but it was a careless thing to do."

"They would have been killed, Tio." Diego said, still teary-eyed from the whole event.

"You're all sewn up, senior Scott," the captain said, ignoring his nephew.

"Thank you, sir," Scott said to the captain, then turned to Diego. "And you, my friend, should live. Unfortunately, you may end up with some nasty scars when it's all said and done."

Diego looked at the stitching on his thigh and calf, concerned. Mel smiled conspiratorially and whispered to him, "Ohhh, most women think nasty scars and their stories are hot. Ariana will love them. You got them for her." Mel nodded with a wink at Diego. Scott felt his heart sink slightly. He didn't have any nasty scars, nor did he have a story about saving Mel. In fact, it was the other way around.

"Don't encourage the boy," the captain said, but with a sly smile. He mussed Diego's hair and walked out the door.

A few minutes later they were back in their dorm room getting out fresh clothes and readying for showers.

"Man, you looked like Lane Frost ridin' dat demon bull!" Scooter howled at Scott.

"Don't think he went eight seconds though," Mel teased, pulling off her soiled shirt, revealing a dirty sports bra.

"Nah, but we're gonna give 'em the Double Backbone Award anyways. He got more guts than you can hang on a fence." Scooter chortled and went into the showers.

Scott had his back turned, acting as if not hearing the banter. He knew it was good-natured, but hearing Mel tease him burned a little.

"Coming in the shower?" Mel asked, popping him on his butt with a rolled-up towel.

"Yeah, I will in a sec," he answered with a forced smile, then turned back to his bunk.

****

The waiting area outside of Director Lott's office was buzzing with activity, aides moving all around, in and out of the hallways and other offices. Phones rang endlessly, and the sound of several conversations was constant. On the walls were photos or paintings of prominent politicians, eagles, and American flags. The great seal of the Intelligence Branch was stitched into the huge plush rug on the floor. Neither Rob nor Dr. Sheltie spoke. Each was wondering about the conversation taking place behind the director's closed door. Masters had been inside for nearly two hours.

Also in the office was the head of the DEA's South American Operations and CIA's director of Clandestine Teams. Rob felt like this was a witch hunt for sure. They probably had their stories all pressed and practiced, pinning everything on Masters. His stomach ached with anxious anticipation. Dr. Sheltie felt the same way. She never felt right about Masters turning himself into the lion's den so feely. He was in no shape to be defending himself right now. She could tell Masters was weary to his bones from the sleep deprivation and now these apocalypse matters. She felt sad she was so hard on him when they first met in her home office. She didn't realize how desperate he was. She thought he was just some burned-out junkie, and him punching her in the face didn't allow her much compassion for him. But now, knowing what she knew about the truth in Belize, or rather vicariously experiencing it, she would certainly fight for his freedom if it came to it. Thinking they were in that office ganging up on him made her furious.

A commotion stirred down the hallway. Several gasps and scuffling feet. Ten armed military police officers stormed into the sitting area and then stopped. They stood awaiting something. Rob and Dr. Sheltie froze, as did everyone else at this abnormal sight. Moments later a loud voice from within the director's office boomed out, "This is complete bullshit!"

"You can't prove anything! This . . . just . . . scare tactic," said another with a harsh laugh. The voices were muffled behind the thick door. Only when they were at a certain volume could the words be made out.

"Is it? You've known my daughter . . . have the audacity to sit there . . . I'll show you . . . for lying to me!"

Rob couldn't figure out whose voices were whose. Any minute he expected to hear a brawl break out. More garbled shouting, then the office door burst open and Director Lett emerged, his face red with rage.

"Lock these scum up, Sergeant!" he barked at the lead officer, breathing heavily. He then followed them back through the door.

"Wait!" Dr. Sheltie jumped up. "It wasn't his fault! He's telling the truth!"

She tried to push her way into the office. One of the MPs grabbed and held her to the side. She struggled against his grip, even kicked his shins and tried to stomp his toes.

"Let me go, you bunch of assholes! He is innocent, damn you!" She continued screaming as she struggled.

Rob just sat stone-still, his eyes wide with shock. In the office, it was a melee. Things were crashing to the floor, and even glass shattered. The officers were grabbing and fighting, trying to apprehend those inside. He couldn't see well enough to find Masters in all of it. Then there was a pop of a taser, then another. Finally, everything quieted except for some groaning and heavy breaths. Two officers marched out the DEA director in cuffs. He seemed dazed as they half dragged and walked him down the hallway. Next out was the CIA's director. He, too, looked dazed and barely able to walk. Rob expected Masters to be next. Instead Trey Lett stepped out, his hair all askew as he straightened his tie.

"Please join us," he said to Dr. Sheltie and Rob, out of breath. The MP holding Dr. Sheltie released her, and she shrugged harshly out of his grip and stomped into the office. Inside, Masters sat in a chair to one side, thankfully, not a salt or pepper hair out of place. He hadn't been involved in the skirmish. However, he looked exhausted nonetheless. Seeing him now made her so relieved.

"Have a seat," Director Lett said, smoothing out his jacket before sitting behind his desk. "I must apologize for that outburst," he said, motioning at the mess the office was in.

Dr. Sheltie and Rob both nodded their understanding.

"Ben and I had a long discussion before I brought the other two gentlemen in. It seems he was able to fill many gaps in the intel I have been receiving for years on the status of my daughter. My sources on the inside of these agencies already confirmed the truth to me about her death some time ago. I was ready to arrest several people, including Ben, when I heard the CIA was hunting him. That prompted me to look into his involvement in the matter further, and I deduced he may be innocent. I wanted to hear what he would tell me if I looked him in the eye and asked for the truth. I am pleased he didn't toe the agency line on this one. Then I wanted him and me both to hear what the agency heads would tell me." He shifted in his seat and crossed a leg. "From what you have just witnessed, you are aware of which story added up and which didn't," he let the silence linger a second.

"So you knew? For how long?" Dr. Sheltie asked with sympathy. It was beyond her comprehension to have known such an atrocity about his own child and keeping it inside. She, too, had borne the burden of hidden secrets about her own children, but none so horrible. The director let out a ragged breath and swallowed.

"A couple years now. Vanessa was my only daughter," he said, now looking around for something and finding it on the floor. He uncrossed his leg, then leaned over and picked it up. It was a picture; the glass was cracked. He stood it on his desk. It was of him holding a dark-haired girl no older than five years old. She was in a princess dress complete with a tiara. He wore a tropical Tony Bahama button-down shirt and khaki shorts. His face and arms were sunburned, yet his legs were bright white like someone who spends all their time in pants. Behind them was the Cinderella castle at the Magic Kingdom in Disney World. They both were wearing huge grins, cheek to cheek, holding each other tight.

"They grow up too fast, and before long they tell you what they will and will not be doing. Like joining the CIA against your better judgment. I encouraged her not to, but she always wanted to be a spy." He let out a breath. "After five years in the agency and more than a couple hairy situations, she agreed to retire and go into law. She was done, Ben," he said, directing his moist eyes at Masters. "After you finished that Venezuelan assignment, she was coming home . . . for good." It was easy to see contempt, anger, and sadness in his gaze.

Masters swallowed hard. "I take the blame, sir. I suggested we stay another night to let the stress of the last several months of being undercover drain away. Had I not . . . and we had left on schedule, then maybe . . ." Masters looked up at the ceiling squinting hard and took in a breath. Then he lowered his head and looked back at the director. "I'm so sorry, sir."

"Nonsense. How could you have known what would happen?"

They sat in silence for another few seconds. Then the director nodded to himself and picked up his desk phone.

"Mary. Bring in the Masters dozier," he barked.

"Yes, sir," she chirped back.

The door opened, and an aide strolled in and handed a thick file to Director Lett. He licked his finger and started flipping through it. He extracted a page and picked up a pen. With it, he scratched his signature and set it aside. Closing the folder, he looked at Masters. No more watery eyes; he was all business again.

"Benjamin Masters, I duly reinstate you to full senior special agent with the CIA, contingent on you taking a temporary assignment reporting to me and me alone. You will have all benefits, salary retro paid, and your pension reinstated as well. Here are your credentials reflecting active duty." He removed a leather wallet, opened it, and laid it on the desk. "I trust you still have your sidearm?"

Masters looked dumbstruck and nodded affirmatively. Both Dr. Sheltie and Rob sat in their seats slack-jawed.

"Good," Director Lett said.

"Sir, may I ask what the temporary assignment is?" Masters asked after a few seconds of recomposing himself.

"Certainly," Lett answered, looking at all three of them in turn. Then his eyes moved back to Masters with raised eyebrows as if the answer should be obvious. "To save the world."

Chapter Twelve

Masters led Dr. Sheltie and Rob out of Trey Lett's office into a long hallway. People were buzzing all around, talking into cell phones and earbuds. He pulled out his own cell phone, one of several burners, and by memory dialed a number. Now exonerated, he felt safe making contact with more of his old teammates.

His call was immediately dumped to voicemail.

"This better be good. I am heading to lunch . . . BEEP," the message on the other end said.

"Bravo, Alpha," he recited, then paused. He hated the last bit of this stupid call sign and tried to casually turn his head away from Rob and Dr. Sheltie before mumbling, "Daddy Issues." Then he hung up. Both Dr. Sheltie and Rob glanced at him, wondering if they had heard him correctly.

"Don't ask," Masters grumbled just as his phone rang in his hand.

He hit the Answer button and put the phone to his ear, but before he could answer, the voice on the other end screamed, "Pops! That really you, man?"

"Hey, Marty. How are ya?" Masters asked, unenthused. Marty was a true prodigy in science and one of the youngest hires ever by the CIA. He had graduated from Harvard when most boys were discovering their first pubic hairs. At one point Marty, on paper, was Masters's adopted son. Not by choice, but by necessity during a mission a few years ago infiltrating a jihadist stronghold under the guise of a children's home in the UK. Marty, because of his youth, was slipped in to perform recon for Masters's infiltration team. It was only for that mission his paperwork was modified to reflect this adoption. Although Marty was brilliant in the lab and had helped Masters in more than one instance in the field, he would rather suffer castration than be Marty's true stepfather. Their relationship was clearly love/hate, to say the least. Marty loved playing up this young son role every chance he got, knowing it got under Masters's cool demeanor. He rarely left his lab, which was connected to his CIA-furnished apartment. He was the quintessential nerd with essentially zero social skills, which nearly blew his cover during the UK mission.

"I'm swell, Daddy. I've missed you so much. When are you coming home? Mommy has a new boyfriend, and Sis is finding love in all the wrong . . ."

"OK, enough with the daddy crap. What do you have for me?" Masters curtly cut him off. Marty could be quite immature and annoying.

"Aww shucks, Dad, so glad to hear your voice too." Marty snickered, feigning rejection, enjoying the banter too much. There was a clattering of computer keys. "OK, fine," Marty conceded and cleared his throat. "But seriously, it is good to hear from you, Ben. I heard the good news. Welcome back to the family."

"Thanks. Word travels fast."

"It's a small family."

Masters put his phone on speaker, then asked into it, "Have you been following this Supermoon Protocol disaster?"

"Who hasn't? I've been performing some experiments of my own too," Marty replied proudly. The sound of shuffling papers then keyboard tapping ensued.

"I figured you would be. Pray tell," Masters said, becoming more anxious by the second.

"The gamma-ray device is continuously revitalizing the molecular structures of the creatures by providing pulsar wavelengths in timed bursts."

"Slow it down, brainiac. And in English this time," Masters instructed.

"The evolved cell structures in the animals containing the DNA are inherently very fragile. Without the maintenance bursts, these animals could revert back to normal to some extent or just die within about ten minutes or so," Marty explained in layman's terms as much as possible.

"So the device is periodically pulsing some kind of repetitive signal, holding the beasts in their viciously evolved form?"

"Bingo, Daddy-o!"

"How do you know this for sure?" Masters asked, now intrigued.

"I've had some of our boys capture a few evolved specimens and bring them into the lab. Oh man, these beasts are vicious as hell. It took twenty times more xylazine in the tranquilizer darts than used for elephants. I even had to mix fentanyl into the cocktail to ensure the beasts would stay down long enough to transport. After drawing labs on them, I still haven't deciphered all the genome mutations. The pattern is crazy complex. The long and short of it is, they have been programmed to target humans, but not necessarily for survival."

"So they are killing humans for the thrill of it?"

"Yes, very similar to how raccoons will attack groups of chickens, for example. The first kill is out of the primal need to feed, but then they actually start enjoying the sport of it. The strategy that goes into it and, if in a group, the teamwork. At this point they just can't seem to stop until the whole flock is exterminated or they are distracted away. Whoever wrote this DNA concoction no doubt had genocide in mind. Quite genius, really."

"Shit," Masters mumbled. Rob and Dr. Sheltie traded a discouraging glance. They rarely, if ever, heard Masters curse.

"How did you learn of the maintenance pulses?" he asked into his phone.

"I took several blood samples and noticed that in some earlier batches, the mutated cells were degenerating. Then on later samples on the same beast, they had regenerated! The newer samples should have degenerated further, but hadn't. So I figured there must be something revitalizing them. After deep rumination, my thoughts went back to the device on the moon. It is still operational, but doing what while in the moon's normal orbit? So I constructed large lead-lined Faraday boxes to go atop the cages the animals were in and , viola! Within minutes some beasts began to morph back toward normality, yet others just died. But either way, they became docile and non-threatening."

"So it's the moon device we have to destroy?"

"Affirmative, Pops. That's the way I see it."

****

The White House conference room was packed. Every chair around the table was taken by the president's senior staff. Along the walls sat the entourages of each cabinet member in attendance, waiting to take notes, research questions, grab coffee, or whatever else their director demanded. On the walls themselves were several LCD screens showing news feeds and closed-circuit cameras of other board rooms. Masters, Dr. Sheltie, and Rob sat directly across from the big man's seat, the president himself. Conversations, clattering of keyboards, and paper shuffling filled the air as everyone awaited his entrance.

The conference room door opened so abruptly, they could feel a vacuum of air rush out of the stuffy room as the president hurried in. Two people seemed to be talking to him at once, followed by a stream of other busy-looking people. Everyone stood immediately as a hush fell over the room. He motioned for everyone to be seated. As he sat, a folder was dropped in front of him. He picked it up and for several minutes read its contents. He then laid it down and eyed all three of the people directly in front of him, starting with Masters, then Dr. Sheltie, and finally Rob, where his gaze lingered. Rob gulped. His throat was dry, and he felt he was suffocating.

"You're Rob Florchett?" he asked in a direct but not unfriendly voice.

"Yes, sir," Rob squeaked, and bobbed his head.

"I understand a great atrocity has befallen your family, and I am ashamed to say your government is responsible. I want to say on behalf of the United States government, please accept my apologies. I have been briefed on your sleeping affliction, and I am deeply disturbed we allowed that to happen to you and your father. And what we did to your grandfather was just a travesty. Those responsible have been taken into custody, and justice will be served. You have my word on that."

"Thank you, sir," Rob said, shocked at the admission and apology. The president then turned to Dr. Sheltie.

"And you, madam, I understand helped cure this boy of his sleeping affliction?"

"Yes, sir," she said meekly.

There was a notable pause, and he narrowed his eyes. They flicked from her to Rob, then back to her. It seemed he was going to say something further but held back.

"I can only imagine how grateful he is that you were able to help him." Then the president turned to Masters.

"Benjamin Masters. So we meet again."

"It's good to see you, sir."

"You as well. The last time we spoke I believe I was just inaugurated, seven years ago." The president forced a weary smile. "Seems like an eternity now with all that's happened since."

Both Dr. Sheltie and Rob seemed surprised the two knew each other and wondered what that relationship centered around. More secrets seemed to mound up around Masters each day.

"Neither of our paths since have been easy ones, sir."

"No doubt about that. Which brings us to why we are here today. I am told you have some new intimate knowledge about what is happening out there with the so-called animal apocalypse?"

"Yes, sir. We know the gamma-ray device on the moon needed to be within the supermoon's range to Earth to start the evolutionary process. However, what we've just learned is that once the initial evolutionary stages are completed, it continues sending additional bursts every few minutes from the moon's normal distance from Earth. This has allowed the molecular process to sustain in the animals. If we disrupt these intermittent bursts, the animals will no longer be a threat to humans any more than before," Masters explained. He went into the deeper details of Marty's testing with lead-lined Faraday enclosures.

"So how are we to herd all the infected animals together?" asked one of the military joint chiefs, thick with skepticism in his voice. "It's impossible to build one of those Faraday boxes big enough."

"I vote we turn our military loose within our borders. Systematically target our densest population centers and secure them. Use armored cavalry battalions and just exterminate these abominations on sight," suggested an Army general. There were several murmurs around the room.

"That won't work, Tom, and you know it. Put your big toys away for just a minute, would you, and listen? From what agent Masters is explaining, we are going to have to destroy that gamma-ray device, plain and simple," argued a woman from one of the remote conference rooms represented on the LCD displays, labeled Secretary of State. The army general sneered and rolled his eyes but thought better of it to retort.

"Agreed. Could we use the air force's HELWS system?" the president asked. He was referring to the Raytheon-engineered High-Energy Laser Weapon System used to destroy enemy drones and other automated aircraft threats instantly around the globe.

"The moon is nearly 250,000 miles from Earth. The HELWS vertical limit is 65 miles above the earth's surface. It's never been effective outside the atmosphere," replied an air force general.

"What about the SBL program the DOD's been touting as operational for the last year?" the president asked, becoming frustrated with the lack of participation in the room. "Why is it I am doing all the thinking here?" he fumed, looking around at nothing but blank faces.

Finally, a stuffy-looking man in civilian clothes spoke up. "I assume you are referring to the Space-Based Laser system?" He shifted uncomfortably in his seat, being put on the spot. "It isn't quite fully operational, sir. It is *mostly* operational."

"And what the hell does 'mostly operational' mean?" the president emphasized his question using air quotes, his face now flushing red with anger.

"It's still undergoing testing. It wouldn't be accurate enough at this stage to hit a device as relatively small as the gamma-ray transmitter."

There was a heavy silence around this group of people who usually spoke just to hear themselves sound intelligent and important. Now, there was not even intellectual drivel being offered. A smooth, velvety voice broke the silence.

"Sounds like we're gonna have to send someone up there to take it out." It was the voice of Masters. The room fell silent again, pondering that idea. Almost simultaneously, each head turned to look at the head of NASA seated at the far end of the table. It took a couple seconds before he realized the attention in the room had shifted in his direction.

"Ha!" he snorted, then composed himself. "I mean, with all due respect, sir, the budget cuts your administration made during your first term in office have crippled our ability to launch any capable rocket for a moon landing. We've had to outsource all of our space travel needs to aerospace companies in the private sector. Even with their help, it would take months to scramble the resources to complete such a mission, as they all are mostly focused on space tourism, not lunar landings," the head of NASA said wincingly. The president looked like he would have a stroke at any second.

"Clear the room!" the president boomed. "Except for you three," indicating Masters, Rob, and Dr. Sheltie.

A few folks stood and started for the exit. Several of the generals froze in place. They seemed puzzled to be commanded in such a way and dismissed ahead of these civilians.

"Now!" he demanded again, slamming his fist on the table. The room finally cleared, and the remote sessions on the LCD screens were terminated. Masters, Rob, and Dr. Sheltie sat there in utter silence as the president stared into the distance as the last door closed. He drummed his long fingers on the huge oak table.

"Please elaborate, Ben," he said, slowing his breathing and turning to Masters.

"I can speak to our old friend Aleksandr at the Kremlin."

The president guffawed at the thought. "My poll numbers are already in the tank this term thanks to Covid. I'll be crucified in the media if the country learns the demise of the human race may have been caused by us and then we have to be saved by the Russians. We've worked so hard to demonize them over the Ukraine invasion, then to turn around to them with our hat in our hands begging for salvation?" The president sighed heavily and rubbed his face. Dr. Sheltie and Rob sat there quietly, unable to believe they were in the same room as this conversation.

"Alek is a weasel. He'd use this to ruin me. As it stands, I am already in my lame duck season, being I have less than a year in office," the President said into his hands, then turned his red-rimmed eyes at Masters. "I was seconds from calling him out in Pakistan. He hasn't forgotten, you know? 'Cause he obviously snubbed me the last time I was at the Kremlin."

"But you didn't call him out. He owes you big for saving his red ass with the Kremlin. Had Putin found out about his under-the-table dealings of nuclear weapons, he could've been executed, and he knows it. He got a huge pass and that. Bet he hasn't forgotten about that either. He could sneak a single spacecraft up there. It's within his purview to direct such a mission to Roscosmos. They are sending rockets on a monthly basis to their new space station. What's one extra launch?" Masters paused to let the seedling of the idea soak in the juices of the president's political brain.

The president scratched at his chin, considering the idea further. "It may be our quickest option, and Russian people are getting massacred in this apocalypse too," he finally said, now coming around to the idea more and more. Before they left the conference room, Masters knew it would morph into the president's own idea, which he was banking on. Even staring human annihilation in the face, a politician worth their own salt could never let a good disaster go to waste.

The president continued scratching his chin, contemplating, and then said, "It has to be completely black. Totally off the books. I am not authorizing this officially, but I will speak to Trey Lett and float my idea by him and tell him you've volunteered. Let him run point man on this."

In other words, let him take all the risk of blow-back and let the president soak up whatever political glory that comes from it, Dr. Sheltie thought to herself.

The president then smacked his hand on the table in finality and stood abruptly.

"Then it's settled and this conversation never happened." the president sternly narrowed his eyes and leaned in on the three of them. They nodded affirmatively.

"Of course," Masters replied with his subtle nod.

Then with the president's best bullshitter's smile, he shook each of their hands.

"Great to see you again, Ben. When all this is over I'll have you up to the Vineyard for some choice whisky and much-needed R&R." With that he strode quickly to the door, then paused suddenly. He turned slowly with a puzzled expression. "And who do you think would take on such a suicide assignment? I doubt Alek would want any exposure by using Russian assets to clean up our mess."

They sat there thinking about this. It was a fair question. Then a rugged smirk formed on Masters's face. "I think I know just the guy," he cooed gently.

"Who?" everyone asked in surprised unison.

****

"Aww, for fuck's sake, Ben," Scooter blurted into his phone. "You mean you want me to fly some Ruskie, second-hand bucket of metric bolts to the galdammed moon? And then do what when I get there?" Scooter laughed, beside himself with disbelief.

He sat on his bunk back in Mexico listening as comical concern, replacing humor, etched itself across his face. Scott and Mel stopped their game of gin rummy at the kitchenette table to listen. Since coming back from the bull escapade, they were making an effort to be more cordial to each other. Although Mel still felt Scott was a chauvinistic brute, she couldn't deny he was still an awfully handsome one.

Scooter shook his head and continued speaking into his phone, "Ben, we've been through some insane shit together, you and me. And you know I love high-flyin' adventure, but to fly a spacecraft?" He hesitated, listening intently to what he was being told, then added, "But, but . . . to the moon?" He listened further to Masters. His resolve evaporated further. Whatever Masters was saying to him was wearing him down to surrender. Finally, with a deep sigh of a crestfallen child, he replied, "Aight then. Lemme get my boots on and grab my porkpie."

The call ended, and Scooter just sat there staring bewildered at his phone like it might sprout fangs and bite him.

"Should I ask what that was about?" Scott asked hesitantly.

Scooter slowly looked over at the two of them like he had just realized they were there and replied, "Pack your tinfoil hats, lil dogies . . . Seems we're gonna go grab some moonbeams to bring home in a jar."

Chapter Thirteen

Dr. Kerr's office was dimly lit, spacious, and sparsely decorated. There was his desk with a couple chairs facing it. Beyond that was a sitting area with two small couches facing each other with a table in between. Each wall of the room was made of a clear polycarbonate thermoplastic material called Lexan. Lexan boasts an impact strength 250 times greater than that of glass and 30 times greater than that of acrylic, a similar thermoplastic. It allows for the severe pressure of deep ocean depths. Outside the office windows were exhibited some of the most beautifully colored coral in the world. Schools of exotic fish and other ocean life went about their business, making the view from the inside breathtaking. His assistant's voice softly announced Cook would be arriving for his usual morning briefing within minutes. Kerr was kicked back behind his huge desk with a remote in one hand and a latte in the other. Each screen projected the horrors and chaos around the globe. But there was one screen his eyes were glued to. On it, two global religious leaders were arguing what the animal apocalypse meant and whose God was responsible for it. On the left was the charismatic leader of the large Protestant group Brethren and Sisters of the Light, Reverend Faygen. His round, ruddy face was perfectly manicured, hair styled to perfection. He talked with his hands, displaying gold and diamond rings squeezed onto his meaty fingers. His loose jowls vibrated with the conviction of his words. On the right was the supreme Islamic scholar, Allamah Al Azhar. He wore a simple white robe and matching kufi prayer hat. His round spectacles were perched on the bridge of his thick nose above his long graying beard. He conveyed a studious, condescending look.

Journalist Tiffany Cross moderated the debate in her usual stylish professionalism. Her beautiful blonde hair framed her elegantly beautiful face and fell softly around her shoulders. Her makeup was flawless. But it was the intelligent seriousness in her eyes that riveted viewers and guests. They were a piercing blue, bluer than any ocean or sky and seemed to radiate brightly when her passion was piqued or when she became annoyed. They held her guests in their place with the understanding that this was her broadcast. They best play by her rules and answer her questions. A true no-nonsense journalist, she was America's favorite shit-kicking reporter. Dr. Kerr turned up the volume:

"So, Reverend Faygen, are you saying what we are seeing with these vicious animals playing out around the world is just the beginning of a larger apocalyptic event?" Tiffany Cross asked pointedly.

"Ms. Cross, I am saying exactly that. At any moment we will hear the first of the seven trumpets described by the apostle John in the first chapter of Revelations just before the heavens open to reign fire upon us," Faygen vigorously answered.

Cross turned to ask Azhar, "Allamah Al Azhar, do you agree with the reverend? That the events unfolding outside our doors now are signaling the end of the world?"

He adjusted himself in his seat. His hands folded together as one would before a lecture of students, then spoke firmly with a thick Arabic accent, "Allah is cleansing this filthy world of the Western infidels by turning their own beasts against them. It is time for Islam to rise up and take back our lands. It is time for Muslims across the world to unite and usher in our culture and laws to crush the unbelievers."

Faygen shook his head in short, quick, back-and-forth motions, giving his soft face a gelatinous look like a quivering bowl of Jell-O. Nearly standing now, he pointed a sausage-like finger at his camera, then retorted, "It's time you, heathen, accept the true Lord God Almighty. That's what time it is. If you keep clinging to that hollow, make-believe prophet, you'll burn in hell for sure! Turn from your wicked ways, blasphemer, and repent!" the reverend said, his voice rising and falling in that evangelistic cadence that stirs crowds. "Time is short, but it's not too late! The signs and wonders are all around you, Azhar!"

Azhar was now gritting his teeth as fire and brimstone spewed from Faygen's mouth. His face twisted into a hard sneer, and he lashed back, "You speak of blasphemy? You invade our holy lands. You deny our laws and culture! Now you've poisoned the beasts of the earth to indiscriminately kill the righteous and unrighteous alike? You arrogant, pestilent swine! All Western infidels must be wiped from existence!" Azhar belted out a triumphant laugh, then leaned into his camera and hissed, "Allah has instructed his devoted believers to immediately do just that! You're right, swine. Your time is short!" Al Azhar said in a menacing tone. His face flushed a deep red in anger, which contrasted brightly against his white robe and hat.

"Gentleman . . . Gentlemen, please, one at a time." Cross struggled as the two leaders verbally took jabs at each other's religions. Now both men were red-faced and pointing fingers into their cameras, yelling over each other.

"Gentlemen, please!" Cross demanded. Seeing they were not paying her any attention, she made a quick slicing motion across her neck and said, "Cut their mics, Eddie." Silence ensued while the two men vibrantly continued arguing, but muted.

"Gentlemen. You're muted. We can't hear you, so please calm down, and we will bring the mics back up." It was Cross's turn to look contemptuous, her blue eyes flaring.

Both men finally began calming and sat back. Faygen looked like he was about to have a double stroke if his blood pressure didn't burst an aneurysm first. Al Azhar was sweating profusely, his round glasses crushed in his fist. His prayer hat sat slightly askew on his head.

Once the order was returned, Cross continued, "Mr. Al Azhar, going back to your statement, and I quote, 'The Western infidels must be wiped from existence and Allah has instructed his devoted believers to immediately do just that,' please explain that further."

"With pleasure. Over the next seven days all the major cities across the United States, the United Kingdom and Europe will experience nuclear and biological attacks. Some through sleeping Islamic warriors carrying out *istishadi* suicide bombings. Others delivered via strategic air strikes from mighty Islamic armies. There are no longer treaties. There are no longer alliances. There are no longer governments. There is only Islam. Allah has called for a complete cleansing of all unbelievers."

Cross's eyes grew as wide as tea saucers, then narrowed. "So I am hearing you correctly, you are directly threatening the West with nuclear attacks?"

"No, Ms. Cross. I am promising it."

Dr. Kerr muted the news broadcast. Cook had entered and taken a seat just before Al Azhar made the threats against the West.

"Wow. That's not good for our return to Eden," Cook said, looking over at Kerr.

"No, it's not. We can't have those throwbacks ruining our Eden before we can return to claim it," Kerr said, his eyes still on the muted TV. "I'll make some calls and see if I can stall this effort somehow. Now, what do you have for me? Clearly, you see time is of the essence."

"We've fixed the docking issue."

"Great! I'll have the members begin boarding immediately. The moon is still in its closest orbit to us," Kerr said, smiling, slipping his reading glasses on and consulting his phone's calendar. "Operating all shuttles, we could have everyone evacuated by the end of the week. Great work!"

"Sir. I would like permission to do a live run alone, without passengers, just to ensure the simulations were accurate. Also, I can prepare the lunar facilities for live-in conditions. Right now everything is in maintenance mode and would need to be brought online."

Kerr contemplated this. Even though the evacuation was behind schedule, he knew it would be wise for Cook to make a solo run to test the docking procedure to calm everyone's anxiety. Several had voiced concerns about the transport pod's reliability, and readying the facilities ahead of time would make the transition much smoother once the guests arrived. He trusted Cook, so he relented.

"You have four days, not a minute longer. It'll also give me some time to work on this Muslim situation."

"Thank you, sir. I will keep you updated," Cook replied graciously. With that, he took his leave and headed straight for the launch room. As he walked, he mentally created the checklist needed for his departure. For a minute, he wasn't sure Kerr was going to allow him one final solo run and was grateful he did. He took pride in his work, and simulations were just that, simulations. Nothing was a sure thing until it was put into action and physically proven. He didn't want to be responsible for these people's deaths, nor did he want to die himself. Again, he reminded himself, he wasn't a true believer in the Planet's Keepers green religion. His motivation had always been the opportunity to use his engineering genius unabated. The more he saw the death and destruction the crazed animals were causing humans everywhere, the more he doubted he could go through with this scheme completely. Another reason he wanted to go on this test mission alone was to decide once and for all where his allegiance was. And if it ultimately was with mankind, he could destroy the gamma-ray device and end this fanatical nonsense.

He entered the cavernous area where the transport pods were stored, maintained, and launched. There were six transport pods total, each carrying twenty passengers with their pets and luggage. Yes, pets. Each family was allowed one, and it was vetted for signs of the mutations. If found, the animal was put down immediately. Years ago, without being given a reason at the time, the Planet's Keepers had been discouraged from feeding their pets anything from the Chow company. Secondly, they were only allowed to have pets that they raised from birth, no rescue animals. There was no way to know if a rescued beast had ever consumed Chow, because Chow was the go-to feed for most kennels and shelters. It was widely donated, and Chow supported every major animal charity around the world. There were thousands of them. None of the Planet's Keepers questioned these things. Coming from Dr. Kerr, they knew better. He had his reasons, and that was good enough if they wanted to inherit the new Eden.

Cook instructed an engineer to ready transport pod #1 for launch within two hours. The transport pods took about two days to reach the moon. Going and coming back alone would use all the allotted days given to him to complete this trip. Very little, if any, time would be had for readying the facilities.

"Nic!" he hollered after the engineer. "Scratch that. I'll be taking the Viper."

The Viper was a sleek, completely blacked-out spacecraft that was designed for lunar security once the moon colony was populated. Dr. Kerr didn't think there would be nuisances there, but when going into the unknown . . . who knew? And when you had the means to build literally any kind of ship you wanted . . . then why not? It was a fun project for his team. An R&D project of a lifetime, they each had said. The body of the craft was shaped in the spirit of Han Solo's Millennium Falcon from the Star Wars franchise and stuffed with all sorts of defensive and offensive goodies, some known to work in space, while others theorized plausible. Those systems needed to be tested too. The Viper ran the same docking program as the transport pods, so Cook would still be able to test the code fix. He would be knocking out several tests during this one trip. Engineering efficiency. That pleased Cook. But the real upshot was that by taking the Viper, it would cut his travel time significantly. He then would have plenty of time to prepare things in the colony. Then maybe, just maybe, he would have enough extra time to take the Viper for a full workout and one last look at the gamma-ray device. Its two-stage thrusters and hydrogen rocket propulsion system could theoretically achieve nearly 40,000 mph once out of Earth's lower orbit. That kind of speed, Cook couldn't fathom. He was beyond eager to experience it.

****

The Russian State Space Corporation's lineage is traceable back to the Soviet space program of the 1950s. Today, known as Roscosmos, it has the world's premiere space training and technology programs, surpassing anything the US currently had about a decade ago. Its headquarters is Moscow, with its mission control center in the nearby city of Korolyov. However, Scooter, Scott, and Mel were heading to a more remote facility. After twelve hours in flight then landing in Moscow, they were loaded into a universal government-issued black SUV with limousine-style seats that faced each other. Their destination was a top secret location in an undisclosed area north of Moscow. The windows were almost completely blacked out and served better as mirrors. Scooter and Mel sat at the windows, and Scott was sandwiched between them on one bench. Sitting across from them on the other were two Russian sides of beef who seemed to have never learned to smile. They could have been twins with their thick black mustaches, furry *ushanka* hats, and black leather gloves. They spoke very little English, and both wore under-jacket sidearms.

Finally, the SUV slowed to a stop. The driver rolled down his window and exchanged Russian words with a guard and handed over an ID. The fresh air was frigid as it blew in from the open window. Mel shivered.

Coming directly from Reynosa, Mexico, they weren't adequately dressed for the occasion.

"Are we in Siberia?" Mel whispered to Scott, suppressing a cold chill.

"No. We are a long way from there yet," Scott whispered back with a chuckle.

"You're not worried?"

"Nope. Not yet."

She felt the machismo resurfacing in Scott. She rolled her eyes and turned to look out the window. All she saw was a weary traveler's unkempt self staring back at her.

"If they load us on a boat now, I know where we are headed," he whispered, leaning into her slightly. Her side was warm against him. He figured she would pull away, but she didn't. He could make snow angels naked with how high his temperature soared from this. Mel could feel his heat too. It was welcoming even if his attitude was not. She didn't press back against him, but she didn't retreat either. Her body temperature also kicked up several degrees as she fought the urge to enjoy his touch.

"Where?" she asked, trying to stay annoyed.

"It's an island on Lake Lama."

"How do you know?"

Scott turned and began to give her that cocky look, but it melted away when their eyes met. He never realized just how purely emerald green her eyes were because they were usually in a confident, suspicious squint. But now they were wide and innocent. Sparkly as diamonds and so beautifully . . . nervous. Scott softened a bit, hoping to ease her anxiety, then answered her.

"Let's just say their version of the CIA has a lot of meetings here," he genuinely explained, hoping to hold her gaze a second longer.

"Until a few days ago, I'd never been out of Dallas." Mel gulped, looking back to the window and wishing she could see through the damn thing.

The SUV passed through the entrance and drove a couple more minutes, then came to an abrupt halt. The side door opened suddenly. One of the Russians seated in front of them motioned them to get out. Scooter grunted something colorful as he slid off the seat and stretched. Scott slid over to get out next, then paused and turned to Mel.

"You good?"

Mel's composure had returned, and she smirked, "Always," and gave him a hard shove to get going.

The cold air blowing off the lake had a harsh bite to it. Scott was correct about them boarding a boat, as he seemed on most things. *Most things*, Mel emphasized in her mind. She wrapped herself in her arms and shivered. Scott noticed and felt bad he had nothing to offer her and wasn't sure if she would appreciate his arm around her to offer his warmth. Scooter ambled forward, ill-affected by the cold, it seemed.

"Smells like Natasha's whore house," Scooter slurred, taking in a deep breath of the rotting fish smell in the air, just loud enough to be intentionally heard. None of the Russians reacted if they had, their heavy boots now stomping onto a long wooden pier at a quick pace. Ahead, docked to the pier, was what appeared to be a small open-air ferry of some kind. As they approached, a woman holding three large, thick mechanic's parkas stepped off the boat. She handed one to Mel. Mel grabbed it and snugged herself into it greedily. It smelled of engine grease and burly sweat, but she didn't care one bit. She pulled up the hood and cinched it tight around her head, leaving just her nose poking out of a furry hole.

Scott took one and shrugged it on, but Scooter put his palm out, refusing.

"No, ma'am. Not into community duds," he said to the lady.

"Don't be a fool. You will freeze on the water," she replied with a thick Russian accent and pushed it into him more firmly.

"Well, ain't you an insistent lil commie."

She was pale with ice-colored eyes. Jet-black hair flooded around her face, out of her parka's furry hood. Her look was firm but held a small bit of patience with Scooter.

"A man's *яйца* are known to freeze together out here, and I hear the thawing process is quite painful," she explained, cocking her head to the side with her tongue in her cheek.

"My what?" Scooter asked, puzzled.

"Your balls, Scooter. She is trying to help you to not freeze your nuts off," Scott translated, impatient from the cold and ready to be underway on the ferry.

"Well, hell. We can't have none of that." He accepted the coat and tipped his hat to the lady. With a flirtatious smirk, she stepped aside and motioned for him to board the ferry.

"Love a gal that minds a man's oysters," Scooter mumbled, slipping past her.

They were seated on a plastic bench seat. The woman boarded behind Mel and brought over a tray with glasses of clear liquid. She perched beside Scooter, extending the tray.

"Vodka?" she offered. "Good to warm you on the inside."

Mel politely declined, as did Scott.

"You gonna sip one first?" Scooter asked, his brow suspicious.

"You think I try poison you?" she responded, playfully astonished.

"Not accusin', but, yeah."

Scott rolled his eyes and sighed. Mel was motionless, cocooned tightly in her parka. The lady cocked her head with a raised brow, staring at Scooter.

"OK, cowboy. You pick one and I drink the other two. This way you pick your poison."

"Pick my poison? Oh, I get dat. You hear her, Scott? Pick my poison? She's a funny lil cuss." He laughed, nudging Scott's side at the humor.

"Yes, I heard her," Scott responded flatly.

"Aight, that one." Scooter pointed to the one closest.

In two quick moves the lady snatched the other glasses and drained them each without hesitation.

"Your turn, cowboy," she indicated, wiping her mouth with the back of her hand. Scooter had traded vodka, bourbon, and even Jägermeister shots countless times in his life. He held his own most times and didn't feel he was a lightweight. All eyes were on him, and to not be outdone by this petite Russian woman, he grabbed his glass and killed it. The burn in his mouth and lips was unexpected, making his sinuses ignite with intense heat. Almost spewing, he had to force himself to gulp the fiery liquid down. Tears streamed down his cheeks, and the burn down his throat was like swallowing lava. Flames danced in his belly, and it felt like he was exhaling fire.

"Hot damn and Hallelujah!!" he proclaimed, shaking his head vigorously back and forth. His cheeks made a comical slapping noise. Everyone on board laughed at his reaction. Even Mel, her cocoon bouncing up and down with her giggles.

"You like it, friend?" the captain yelled back, looking in his rearview mirror with a deep chuckle, holding up his own drink.

Scooter coughed and wheezed.

"Yeehaw! Now that's what I'm talkin' 'bout. Set us up again, sweetheart!" Scooter demanded, slipping his arm around the lady and pulling her close. She poured them both another round. Scooter scooped his up and held it high for a toast,

"To my fellow comrades!" then gulped down the liquid fire.

Chapter Fourteen

The conference room was quiet, save for the tap, tap, tap of Trey Lett's Mont Blanc pen against the table's hard surface. Masters had just explained Marty's theory about the maintenance pulses keeping the DNA mutations active. He followed it up with the "president's" plan about borrowing a Russian spacecraft to destroy the gamma-ray device on the moon. Lett was silently mulling all this information over.

"Alek wouldn't provide us a pilot for the mission?" Lett asked.

"No, sir. Not to fly the mission, but yes to a pilot to train our guy. He felt he owed us access to a craft, which he says may still be impossible on such short notice. But he couldn't ask one of his team to lead a suicide mission, his words not mine, without word getting out about any of it to the Russian leadership," Masters explained.

"Do *you* believe it is a suicide mission?" Lett pointed his gaze at Masters.

"I believe the best chance at success is in the team we are sending, sir," Masters aptly responded. Dr. Sheltie and Rob looked at each other with deep concern. Neither of them was excited that Mel was going on the mission, but Mel adamantly said she was. She refused to speak further about it on the phone call when Rob laid into her about the sheer danger. No one was in a position to stop her, and there wasn't time to keep trying to persuade her otherwise. Scooter, Scott, and Mel had to get on board the flight from Mexico to Russia immediately. The captain's Learjet had returned from Washington, DC, and was fueled and ready, waiting for them on the tarmac.

"So what is the timeline?" asked Lett, leaning back with his arms behind his head, still contemplating the whole thing.

"I've confirmed they have landed in Moscow and are en route to a remote Roscosmos training facility where they will learn to fly the spacecraft. It should take them a couple of days to get the most basic training.

However, it really depends on how long it takes our pilot to get a handle on flying it."

"And how long until your guy gets a handle on it?"

Masters thought about it and said, "Not long. I've never seen him stumped behind the stick of anything that flies."

****

"You're kidding me?" Scooter looked over at the ice-colored eyes of Nakita Shakalov. It turned out, not only was she the bartender and Scooter's drinking comrade on the riverboat cruise the night before, but she was also a Russian pilot and cosmonaut. A very decorated one at that. Scooter was in disbelief. She was the pilot tasked with training him on the flight basics of the Russian spacecraft assigned for this mission, the Kosmos 2530. Because it was on such short notice, they were authorized to use the only craft that was fueled and ready. The 2530 wasn't the easiest craft to fly, but it was proven reliable. The Kosmos spacecraft would be launched into orbit by the new Russian prototype Angera 2 rocket system. The Angera 1 rocket system had been in use for nearly a decade moving people and supplies to the Russian Space Station, but never beyond. The Angera 2 rocket propulsion system had been designed for travel beyond the space station, but it was untested.

"I am supposed to control this steroid-pumped rocket with a vintage Atari controller?" Scooter was referencing the small AIRLink controller built into the flight simulator's control board. It reminded him of the joysticks he used with computer games as a kid in the 1980s. He was starting to even more regret Masters talking him into this.

"The spacecraft runs on autopilot. The joystick controller is mostly used for docking and landing maneuvers. I highly doubt you will need to actually steer the craft during flight. Not much to run into up there," Nakita explained. "But you need to learn just in case of autopilot failure. You would still have to get home."

"Naturally," Scooter mumbled, looking around as he continued to take everything in. She said something in Russian into her headset, then turned to Scooter, "We will be speaking in English for the training."

"Thank you. My Bolshevik is a bit rusty," he replied dryly.

"Control, this is Regal 3," she said in accented English into her headset.

"Regal 3, copy," the control room replied.

"Clear to begin simulated launch sequence."

"Roger that. Commencing sequence."

In Scooter's ears he heard a backward countdown from ten begin. Nakita began flipping this switch and that one, pressing buttons and dialing in certain things.

"The simulation is pretty realistic. It should feel like we are pulling four to five g's before breaking the earth's atmosphere," Nakita explained.

"Ain't no biggie," he answered more boldly than he actually felt. Just sitting there caused his stomach to do flip-flops from all the vodka the night before. He wondered how she could be so ill-affected by it. She must've been drinking since birth to have that level of alcohol tolerance.

The voice finished the countdown, "Three, two, one . . . ignition."

The simulator began a grumbling shake as the rockets ignited. Slowly it began to feel like it was launching. The g forces started to build evenly but quickly. Scooter's stomach lurched up in his throat, then slammed down in his gut as the simulation picked up speed.

"Awe, man. Any barf bags in here?"

****

Mel and Scott had been taken into another room. In here there was a huge tank of water that resembled a massive aquarium. Positioned in front of it was a control desk with three technicians seated, working on computers. Mel and Scott would be tasked with destroying the gamma-ray device once Scooter brought the craft into range on the moon. Nikolav Sashavik was one of the technicians at the control desk. He was monitoring the tank's controls and led the training exercise. In the tank were Mel and Scott, both outfitted in the latest space apparel. Nothing like those worn during the Apollo missions, these were thin and form-fitting. The helmet was smaller and contoured their faces. Weighted belts had been fitted around their waists to

199

neutralize buoyancy. This gave them the feeling of a zero-gravity environment.

"This is pretty cool!" Scott said as he slowly maneuvered a summersault.

"Show off!" Mel laughed, and proceeded to do one in reverse. They continued getting used to zero gravity when Nikolav's voice spoke into their comms.

"OK, cosmic acrobats. Let's get to the training. We are going to increase the weights in your belts to bring you to the level of the moon's gravitational pull. It is about one-sixth of the earth's. You will start being pulled to the bottom of the pool. The bottom simulates the moon's surface," the voice explained. Slowly Mel and Scott began to sink to the bottom of the tank.

"We have been sent schematics of the gamma-ray device from our consul in the US. You should see a fairly accurate replica there to your right. Next to it is a set of tools you will use to disable it," Nikolav instructed them on the process of taking the device offline.

"You must never be in front of the directional dish. The gamma rays would pass through you with such force you would be incinerated. The rear of the device should be adequately shielded, as it was designed as such for the installation of the unit."

Mel visualized herself being blasted into billions of ionic particles and wafting away into space like dust. The danger began to set in on Mel. Up until now she had seen this as an adventure.

"Next to the directional dish are the solar collectors. These power the device and collect the necessary spectral radiation from the sun to create the rays and shoot them to Earth. You will need to sever this link by using the provided cutters. They are heavily insulated to protect you from being shocked. There is plenty of voltage to kill you, so be careful," Nikolav warned.

Scott started to sweat in his suit. He wondered what the success rate for such a mission was. In the field as a CIA agent, these calculations were given to the agents in the briefing before an assignment. It ensured they appreciated the seriousness of what lay ahead. He figured this mission could be rated less than 50/50, substantially less. Mel removed the access panel and disconnected the capacitor boards. Once done, Scott exhaled slowly as he followed Nikalov's instructions and applied pressure to the cutters. The strong pneumatic jaws slowly chewed through the cable until they clamped closed. The cable fell into two pieces.

"That's it?" Scott asked.

"That's it for that part," Nikolav answered.

"Should've known there was more," Scott groaned, peeking over at Mel, who was intently watching him with her solar shield up. Her emerald eyes shimmered in her helmet, full of concentration.

Nikolav walked them through the rest of the steps to render the device offline.

"It's been fifty years since this thing was installed. I doubt the conditions of it will be exact. The blueprints aren't as detailed as I had hoped for, but the gist of everything is to simply power it off."

"How will we know for sure if we succeed in doing that?" Mel asked.

"I am not a hundred percent sure. I have no information here on control boards, switches or key point indicators to look at. It is a very crude yet very effective device," Nikolav replied.

Mel looked stressed, worried. Now her suit and this tank were becoming very claustrophobic. Scott, too, had a sinking feeling about everything. They would only get one shot at this for all mankind. The fate of the world was literally on their shoulders.

****

"Are you ready to take over?" Nakita asked Scooter as the simulated separation of the spacecraft and rocket assembly completed. His squishy stomach had settled a bit, and he began to feel more like himself. Nakita was gliding the craft around smoothly. It looked straightforward to him. No wind to contend with; hell, there wasn't even a gravitational pull. Nothing like fighting the yoke on a vintage Huey or ripping through jungles or deserts in a heavily equipped Apache. Besides, the little Russian butterfly seated next to him was only rotating her wrist and daintily tapping her fingers on a video game controller while they buzzed smoothly around this simulated universe.

"I was born ready," Scooter replied.

"Remember, you will need to fight your terrestrial flying instincts. It's a totally different world up here. There are no rudders, wind currents, or wing flaps.

203

Propulsion is your steering. Timing your forward, aft, and tertiary thrusters in concert is the key," Nakita cautioned.

"I hear ya, sister," he replied.

"Regal 3 requesting permission to hand control over to John Wayne," Nakita said into her comm unit. Scooter didn't realize he had a radio handle assigned to him. He looked over and sucked in a proud breath.

"The Duke? I like it," he said with a wry smile.

"I thought you would. Now take me cruisin', cowboy," she said, her lip in a half smile Scooter thought was way too damn sexy.

"Roger that, Regal 3. John Wayne has control," the disembodied voice broadcasted. The simulator immediately began spinning wildly like a top.

Chapter Fifteen

The Viper sat attached to one of the three-stage rocket systems built to launch from the unique underwater tube. A catapult system, similar to one on an aircraft carrier that slung fighter jets into the sky, would sling the spacecraft up the tube and then through a hundred or so feet of water. Once free from the ocean's surface, the rockets would engage. The craft's sophisticated computer system would keep the tube pointed skyward. There would be a few seconds in which the catapult's inertia would start to decrease before the thrusters took over. The process resembled a bottle rocket that has been tossed into the air a few seconds before the fuse ignites the powder. The three stages of the rocket system would fire sequentially through the earth's atmosphere into space. Once in space, the Viper craft would separate and continue the journey to the moon using its own hydrogen-fueled propulsion system.

Rodnell Cook sat inside, readying the controls. The steering mechanism was more traditional on the Viper. It was like a race car wheel versus a joystick. The propulsion system was far more advanced than the Russian Kosmos 2530. Its rocket thrusters were tied to the steering wheel's left and right movement, making navigation more intuitive. There were even pedals that worked similarly to gas and brake pedals on a car.

"All onboard systems are online," Cook said into his comm mic.

"Roger that. Still bringing the catapult system up to full thrust," replied the launch engineer.

Cook sat back and tried to relax his breathing. He knew he would need his adrenaline at a minimum level during the initial phases of the rockets. This system pulled a few more g's than both the Russian rockets and the passenger pods. His g suit was fitting snugly. Its design was to apply pressure to his legs and torso using built-in airbags to keep the blood from rushing into his extremities. Fighter pilots used them to help them not lose consciousness pulling major g's in a skirmish. Once out of the earth's gravitational pull, he would slip into his space suit for the remainder of the trip.

"Catapult is fully charged. Awaiting the last launching checkoff to complete," the voice said in his ear.

For several years, engineers and enviro-physicists had been making this trip back and forth to build out the lunar community. The materials used in its construction were all soft materials created in the Planet's Keepers laboratories. Once assembled, they resembled very large pup tents. Each was connected by tunnels constructed of the same materials. Self-sustaining, perpetual air and water filtration with electrical and sewage technology with redundant backup systems were built into their designs. Some tent-looking structures served as large agricultural centers, equipped with exclusive grow-light technology, using aquaponic growing pools. Aquaponics is the blending of hydroponics and live fish. In this system the fish would create fertilizer for the plants and also serve as a protein source for the community, as their diet would consist mostly of plants. The entire effort was concealed by the moon's synchronous rotation with Earth's, creating the dark side of the moon effect in which the lunar community lay hidden.

Cook completed a three-month tour a year back. While there, he mostly performed technology installations and inspections. Since returning to Earth, he had been very eager to go back. Being there was an amazing feeling. The views were beyond words. Returning to the colony solo, behind the wheel of the Viper, his thrill level exceeded any measure.

"Ready to initiate the countdown, sir," the voice reported.

"Let's rock and roll," Cook replied, feeling the jolt of the catapult arm secured to the rocket. He took in a deep breath and gripped the handles on the side of his seat. The catapulting experience was intense. Even though it lasted just a couple seconds, the gravitational force was beyond any thrill ride's capabilities. It literally pinned the pilot completely to the seat, unable to breathe until the spacecraft cleared the ocean's surface.

"Three, two, one . . . engage."

There was a click, and then a huge invisible hand pressed hard against Cook's chest. His cheeks pulled back, showing his teeth in a strained grin. A grunting noise came from his throat. Then there was the noise of fast-rushing water, then silence. His chest expanded, taking in air. He could hear his blood rushing in his ears. Suddenly the invisible hand returned, pressing him into the seat once more. This time it was not as intense, but breathing took effort. The roar of the rocket's first stage was deafening. Straight ahead was pure sky, light blue turning darker by the second. The deafening rocket ceased suddenly as the second phase kicked in. The invisible hand lessened its pressure on his chest, and he was able to inhale almost normally.

"How are you doing, Viper?" the voice in his ear said. Cook adopted the craft's name as his call sign.

He swallowed and exhaled slowly. "All good. Systems look good. Operating normally," he responded.

"Nice," the voice replied. "Looks good from here too. Sit back and enjoy the ride. The computer should take you the rest of the way and dock automatically."

Cook hoped the bug was truly fixed, or the docking effort might be the last thing he remembered.

****

"Counter the spin with the stick!" Nakita instructed.

"I am!" Scooter snapped. He felt he was about to break the little joystick off the control panel. The more he tried to correct their trajectory, the more the ship spun. "Aww hell!" Scooter yelled as the craft started tipping forward into a somersault.

"Regal 3 requesting control," Nakita requested.

"Roger that, Regal 3 has control."

Slowly, the craft began to slow its spin until it finally leveled out. Sweat was running down Scooter's brow. He wiped his sleeve across his forehead. They sat in silence for a couple minutes, catching their breath. Nakita could see the frustration on Scooter's face and felt it better to not say anything, let him process what had happened, what mistakes he may have made and how to correct them next time.

"You were right," he turned and said to her.

"I was?"

"It definitely is a whole new experience," he said somberly.

"No one does well the first time," she replied, and placed her hand on his and leaned into him slightly.

"It's like making love." She smirked. "The more you learn about your partner, the better it gets."

Scooter hiked his eyebrows, unsure whether the partner in her analogy was her or the spacecraft. Before he could ask her to elaborate, the simulator's door opened and a technician stepped in and began adjusting some knobs in the rear control center. He said something in Russian with a laugh. She replied back in kind to the technician, then looked at Scooter and said, "Set us up to start again. John Wayne is going to get back on his horse."

****

At least with the threat of nuclear attacks across the US and Europe, the twenty-four-hour news cycle had something else to exploit. Dr. Kerr sat at his desk wondering what the best approach would be to stave them off. Pundits and reporters were now focused on which cities they predicted would be attacked first. Paris, New York City, and London were at the top of their list. The animal apocalypse was now becoming yesterday's news.

If even one nuclear detonation occurred, it might change the Planet's Keepers plan, although unlikely.

However, if numerous detonations occurred, it certainly would. It would take the earth decades, maybe even fifty years, to recover from the nuclear winter that would ensue, delaying their return to Eden beyond their limits and supplies on the moon. The plan was to maintain their colony on the moon for a year, maybe two, tops.

Dr. Kerr picked up his cell and began browsing his contacts. Everyone from the rich and famous, presidents of past and present, and dictators to dignitaries, royalty, and business moguls were scrolling before his eyes. One group of people he never had great success influencing was the radical Muslims. He hated speaking with them for several reasons. They certainly had zealots in their fold, but none of them were committed to environmental causes. They didn't have a pop culture leader. In fact, most of the world couldn't name one Muslim leader outside of Osama Bin Laden, and he was long gone. They cared little for money unless they needed to fund a jihad, and would sacrifice themselves in the name of martyrdom. Their focus was always to destroy the West. Period. Most every other government, group, or race of people had bent the knee to Mother Earth, giving Dr. Kerr clout within their ranks.

If he needed to curry favor, it was easy to locate the appropriate contact to bribe or influence. It was rare he was at a loss to devise a plan. He needed someone the radicals would listen to, someone that could slow down this nuclear exuberance. Only one name came to mind, and it turned his stomach.

He paused his scrolling and clicked that name, then punched the Call button. After three rings it was answered.

"Assalam alaikum. May peace be upon you, Dr. Kerr," the voice greeted him.

"Wa alaikum assalam. And peace be upon you," Kerr replied back.

"I was wondering when I might hear from you," king Abdullah bin Abdulaziz of Saudi Arabia said in perfect English.

"Why is that?"

"Given the state of the world currently, of course. I'm sure you are aware of the nuclear threats being plastered across the headlines."

"Hard to miss right now."

"Funny thing, when I first read them, I actually thought of you first."

Dr. Kerr doubted the king had learned of the threats the same way as everyone else. No one was more connected to radical Islam than King Abdullah. Dr. Kerr didn't ask why his name popped up first in the king's mind. The king often spoke in riddles, compelling the other person to keep asking, "Why?" "Why?" "Why?" It fed his ego of being the one with all the answers.

The king waited for a beat. When Dr. Kerr didn't bite, he said, "Nuclear detonations, one would think, are at the top of your list of potential travesties humans could commit against your precious planet."

Dr. Kerr bristled but kept his voice calm and even. The king's arrogance was known far and wide.

"*Our* precious planet," he corrected the king.

"At least for today, yes," the king retorted dismissively.

"So can you help in this matter? Intervene and bring some sanity to this situation?"

"I wish I could. Nuclear winter is not something I would delight in personally. However, this is something even I can't stop."

"I find that hard to believe, knowing what I know about you," Kerr replied, trying to keep his temper in check.

"Knowing what you know about me is the only reason you have this number and why I answered your call. Don't be a fool to think that knowledge gives you any leverage in our conversations," the king replied, his jovial tone turned icy.

Dr. Kerr felt he needed to step back a bit and try more diplomacy. "You're right. Accept my apologies."

"I understand you are passionate about your cause. But Islam is passionate about ours too. You know we have itchy fingers when it comes to bombs. And the itchiest of them all are on nuclear devices. As a culture we have awaited this moment for what seems an eternity."

"And what moment is that?"

"A unification of all Muslims sparked by a common atrocity by the West," the king explained. The conversation stalled for a minute.

"I think we can help each other out," said Kerr.

"Now you are speaking a language I understand," the king said. He sat back in his chair to listen. He knew Dr. Kerr was a man of connections, action, and means.

But the king didn't need money. He had more wealth than most global economies. He wanted information, information that led to the demise of the West. Dr. Kerr knew this and explained his proposition. What did it matter if he showed cards that he normally would hold close? The King, Islam, and all humans would be annihilated within the year anyway.

Chapter Sixteen

Newly reinstated CIA agent Benjamin Masters left the office of National Security director Trey Lett, no longer on the run, but in pursuit. Beside him walking briskly was Dr. Sheltie and Rob.

"We need a plan B. I know you have full confidence in Scooter, but what if they fail?" Dr. Sheltie asked. Then looked at Rob and said, "Not that I think they will."

Rob's lips were pressed tightly together, and he only nodded he understood. But in his head he knew failure was Mel's death sentence. He needed to find a way to help her any way he could.

"I agree. Any ideas?" Masters replied.

"We need to find out who is behind the Chow company and what their plan is. This is all too calculating to be some coincidence."

"One step ahead of you," Masters said as they entered the elevator and he pushed the ground floor button. "I have Marty working on that. He is tracing the catalytic ingredients in Chow's recipes to their origins. Doubtfully these types of ingredients are easy to obtain, and some we're not even sure occur naturally. They probably would need to be manufactured in a lab using a very dangerous production method. We find these sources, we find our mastermind." The elevator doors closed on three very determined faces.

****

The following day was dedicated to more rigorous training for Mel, Scott, and Scooter. They each had spent the last sixteen hours straight sharpening their efforts for disarming the gamma-ray device and flying the spacecraft. Scooter had graduated from needing Nakita in the cockpit with him, although he would admit he had dragged his feet just a tad in his improvements to keep her at his side a bit longer. He had become infatuated with her, and he hoped she was with him too. The night before, they had shared a late dinner together in the mess hall. No vodka this time. Their apt attention was all too important in the coming days.

Even without vodka, they enjoyed each other's company, sharing stories of wild tales in flight. Scooter was shocked to learn they nearly crossed paths in the sky back a few years ago during a dustup in extreme Northern Pakistan. The Russians were covertly moving a small nuclear payload across a small sliver of Afghanistan. The destination was a small outpost in Pakistan. During the crossing they were ambushed by Al-Qaeda forces and the payload was stolen. Aleksandr Antonov, head of Russian weaponization technologies and some other non-military programs, such as Roscosmos, had ordered the delivery without official authorization from the Kremlin. He thought he had bribed the appropriate officials in Afghanistan and later learned he was double-crossed. Antonov would have received a tidy sum of cash from the Pakistanis upon a successful delivery. The nukes were from a Cold War stockpile and wouldn't be missed. However, had the Kremlin learned of the debacle, it would have meant his life.

United States Special Forces were training the local Afghan army at a base Northeast of Kabul,

Afghanistan. Antonov had no choice but to discreetly ask for assistance through secret channels. A small group of CIA and Navy SEALs made their way north to meet another small group of Russians. Nakita was a pilot within the Russian group. However, the US assets got there first. They found the Al-Qaeda contingent and took them out, gaining possession of the nukes. Scooter provided transportation and air cover in a DARPA-modified Apache helicopter for the US team. The whole skirmish lasted just ten minutes, and the US and Russian teams never actually met.

Antonov politely asked for the nuclear ordinances back from the US forces. The then first-year US president was called and briefed for direction. This was an awfully large favor the US had done for Antonov. The president wanted quid pro quo, so he sent CIA operative Benjamin Masters to a secret meeting with Antonov to be his in-person liaison to negotiate a deal. There wasn't much Antonov claimed he could negotiate. However, the president felt otherwise and threatened to blow the whistle on Antonov. After several days of intensely heated conversation between the president and Antonov, Masters was able to discourage any leaks of the situation and was able to have the nukes covertly dismantled and destroyed. This left the president and Antonov at odds with one another, and nothing more had happened since, until the favor called into Antonov a day ago about loaning the US team a spacecraft. Antonov was in no position to deny the favor.

Together, sharing both sides of that story, Nakita and Scooter had built a bond. They decided to toast their new friendship with a single shot of vodka before heading to bed. Both lay awake thinking of the other as they drifted off to sleep in their individual beds. The next morning it was go-time.

****

Rodnell Cook had docked the Viper at the loading platform of the moon colony with ease. The adjustment the Kid made in the coding algorithm allowed for flawless execution. No gaps in the air lock. A perfect seal. For the last day he had been bringing all stations and support systems out of maintenance mode to fully online. His suit was getting stuffy and annoying. There were ten minutes left on the display until he could remove his space suit and breathe the air within the living areas. It took the oxygen HVAC systems twelve long hours to bring the place to non-spacesuit status. He hadn't been able to sleep while wearing it, so he decided to power through his system preparation checklist. Once he was able to take it off, he would grab some much-needed sleep.

He stood in front of a large window and gazed out into space. It never failed to take his breath away. Such infinite blackness and the stars, when viewed from here, were much more clear and brilliant than anywhere on Earth. He could take in this view forever. He loved it here. So peaceful, so isolated. At this moment he was the only human being on this vast moon. The thought of how he could be so blessed boggled his mind. He had Dr. Kerr to thank, and he would once he returned. All the frustrations of the past decade were finally receding. They were within just days of finishing this phase, and no one was more ready than Rodnell Cook. Dr. Kerr had become a touch overbearing the last couple of weeks. But that was understandable considering the feat at hand.

A buzzer sounded, waking him from his daydream. He walked over to the HVAC control board and saw the green light indicating it was safe to discard his space suit. Even though he trusted his computers and their programs built by his team, he always was nervous about the initial unlatching of the seal of his headgear. He pressed the safety off its lock, but hesitated before unlatching it. He laughed at himself for being nervous. He yanked the latch open, and his suit exhaled its internal pressure. He slowly breathed in a breath, waiting for the burn of oxygen starvation in his lungs. He exhaled and breathed in again. No burn, just sweet oxygen. He quickly took the suit off and stowed it. He double-checked all the control boards in the room. Green lights all around. The moon colony was online and ready to receive its inhabitants. He locked the door and made his way to the kitchen area and pulled out a couple MREs, boiled some water, and blended everything together in the correct proportions.

He sat at the end of a table in the dark-and-quiet cafeteria enjoying his dinner. Afterward, he would grab a shower, find a suitable bunk, and sleep for six hours. Then he would mix some strong coffee, shower again, and load back into the Viper. But he wouldn't be returning to Earth just yet. He had earned himself half a day to circle the moon and test the Viper's full propulsion and weapons systems. He hoped his anticipation would allow him to fall asleep. With his belly full and the soft mattress caressing his weary body, he did so within minutes.

****

Masters, Dr. Sheltie, and Rob had begun doing research on the origin of the Chow company. They had set up their laptops in a secure room that had access to the CIA's network. Now having access to the CIA's records and databases, they could follow the timeline from when Chow was originally purchased from the Texas owner and moved to Maryland by the CIA. Then in 1973, it sold to another entity when the Supermoon Protocol project was pulled by Richard Nixon just before the signing of the Paris Peace Accords ending the Vietnam War.

"There is very little information on the buyers," remarked Dr. Sheltie.

"Buyers? Like there were more than one?" Rob asked.

"It has changed hands a few times since, yes."

"What info is there?" Masters walked over, now interested.

"Well, in '73 it was purchased by a shell corporation, then transferred its ownership to another company through a stock liquidation. That company's name isn't here in these records. Just the signature of an F. S. Kerr."

"F. S. Kerr . . . F. S. Kerr," Masters repeated the name, deep in thought. "Why does that name sound familiar to me?"

"Kinda sounds like that environmental evangelist with the Planet's Keepers," Rob said. "The Planet's Keepers have chapters on every major university campus. I wrote several articles on them when I was the college newspaper editor in Texas. A very passionate bunch."

"But that's Warwick Kerr. Dr. Warwick Kerr. Not, F. S. Kerr," Masters said thoughtfully.

"I wonder if there is any relation?" Dr. Sheltie wondered aloud as she brought up a Google search on her laptop. Several hits came up for F. S. Kerr. She clicked on the Wikipedia link.

"Get this, F. S. Kerr is Franklin Scott Kerr . . . The original Planet's Keepers founder. Dr. Warwick Kerr is his son and the current leader of the group. Seems Franklin Kerr passed away about five years ago," Dr. Sheltie read aloud.

The cell phone in Masters's pocket vibrated. He pulled it out and looked at the ID. It read Marty. He was eager to hear his findings but knew he would have to go through the same tiring daddy charade.

"What do you have for me?" he asked, hoping to get to the point.

"Nice to hear your voice, too, big poppa."

"Cut the crap. This is too important." Masters sighed irritably.

"Right, right . . . no sense of humor. Anyways, I have made *progress* for you. What else would you expect?"

"I'm listening."

"Gotta hand it to the Germans. They are the experts on simple yet effective."

"Explain, please."

"I expected the catalytic ingredients to be complex. However, they aren't really ingredients at all. All the gamma-ray is doing is unstabilizing certain atoms in the animal's genome through electroporation, then inserting DNA sequences of heightened sensory and growth hormones stored in the food. When digested, the new sequences lie dormant inside the animal's body until the atoms become unstable. The unstable atoms give off excess energy and mass which absorb the new hormones. This is the catalyst for the changes in the animals. The atoms then stabilize, but the new stable atoms can't sustain under the demands of the mutated genome, so the gamma-ray device sends another destabilizing pulse, and the cycle repeats. And this goes on and on until the gamma ray stops the pulses or the physical body of the beast deteriorates, which I am guessing, could take weeks, maybe even months."

"Interesting, but we don't have weeks or months," Masters said, concentrating hard to jump to Marty's conclusion. "What does this tell us other than why the gamma-ray device sends out the maintenance pulses?"

"Well, I thought that was a pretty amazing find in and of itself because this was not how the gamma-ray device was designed. After the supermoon moved back into its normal orbit, the evolutions were supposed to cease, like in the animals in my earlier experiments with the Faraday box. So somehow someone has found a way to modify it to perpetuate its effects on the animals longer term."

"Any idea who or how?"

"The modification would have to have been done to the gamma-ray device itself. From the engineering schematics, I don't see any remote access capabilities. It is a pretty rudimentary device," Marty replied.

"You mean someone physically went to the moon to make the modifications?" Masters asked, totally perplexed.

"The best I can tell, yes."

"Who has the means or even the knowledge to do that?"

"I'm still working on that."

"Get back with me when you have something on *that*." Masters ended the call and returned his attention to Dr. Sheltie's screen. She and Rob were reading through the news articles on the Planet's Keepers, hoping to find some kind of connection to the Chow company.

"Here's something interesting. In 1980 the Chow company joined in a partnership with a new animal rights group. This new partnership had a pretty big sponsor behind it right out of the gate: the Planet's Keepers," Dr. Sheltie said. She turned to Masters and said, "Guess which animal rights group it was?"

"I'm not up on my animal rights groups, so I wouldn't know." Masters said, puzzled.

"Environmentalists for the Rights of Animals. The E-R-A," Dr. Sheltie said slowly, allowing this nugget of info to settle in on the group.

"You mean that wacked political group that stages all those outlandish protests?" Rob asked.

"Bingo."

"My God. They are all over the world," Masters breathed.

"Yep. Spreading the good word of Chow. It wasn't until the mid-'80s that Chow exploded globally as a household name. They can thank the ERA for fueling the outlandish conversations that allowed Chow to capitalize on them," Dr. Sheltie added.

"Controversy is the best marketing tool, and not many groups out there are as controversial as the ERA," Rob said as he searched YouTube for ERA rallies. Sure enough, the Chow brand was everywhere in the videos—

on T-shirts, banners, and even superimposed on some of the videos themselves.

"And now we have a pretty good idea who owns the Chow company," Masters said.

"Dr. Warwick Kerr," they all said in unison.

Chapter Seventeen

Dr. Warwick Kerr walked out of the engineering lab and down the underwater plexiglass hallway to his office. He was smiling to himself. The conference call with Rodnell Cook moments ago delivered splendid news. The docking procedure glitch was fixed. Cook had all systems at the moon colony online and functioning normally. He should be heading back to Earth this evening. Then his apostles and their families could begin boarding. The only issue that needed to be wrapped up was this nuclear threat business. His conversation with the king had gone better than he expected.

A little confidential leak of backdoor accesses to the US and European power grids and major waterway systems was a small price to pay to stop the earth from nuclear destruction, right? Who knows, when I return to claim the new Eden, I may decree myself a savoir of sorts. A prophet or saint. Something surely to raise my stature among my apostles and closer to Mother Earth herself, he thought as he entered his office. Dr. Kerr came by this access to power grids and such through one of his companies that installed several large solar and wind farms in the US and abroad. They required this access to integrate these farms into these main government-run entities. He was bound by contracts and some laws not to share that information with anyone. Laws and contracts would be useless to uphold by the end of the year. Courts and governments would be obsolete, so he had no worries. He noticed across one of his flat-screen TVs there was a breaking news bulletin.

"Ah, Ms. Tiffany Cross, what have you got for me today, gorgeous?" he asked the TV as he turned up the volume:

"This just in. Breaking news in the Islamic global nuclear threat situation. An anonymous message was distributed across several of the major social media platforms today, saying, 'Islam has finally found the way to destroy the Great Western Satan. We find no need to punish our own righteous believers with nuclear fallout. We have discovered a way to focus our retribution in a less destructive yet equally disastrous way to the infidel swine. All true believers of Islam should flee these Western lands or be swept up in Allah's wrath. Glory be to him and him alone!'

"No single group has claimed responsibility for this message, although it does seem credible, as many nuclear-capable Muslim countries have stood down their defenses and weapons from DEFCON 1 to DEFCON 3 or equivalent.

"What does this new message mean for Western countries? Who was able to broker this deal with Islam? Lots of questions and rumors are swirling around. But the world is breathing a small sigh of relief as the nuclear rhetoric seems to be dialing back. We will continue to watch the situation closely. This is Tiffany Cross reporting. Back to you in the studio, Eddie."

Dr. Kerr's smile broadened as he leaned back in his chair. He should have tried to recruit Tiffany Cross to the Planet's Keepers. He could use her brains and that body to keep him company on the moon colony. *Maybe I do need to bring a companion along.* As his mind drifted, putting together a short list of lucky candidates, his phone beeped a text alert. It was from his cybersecurity team.

These alerts were never good. He opened his text app and read:

> **Cyber Tech:** We are picking up traffic on our public-facing subnets originating from IP addresses we know to be used by the CIA and NSA. Please advise.
>
> **Kerr:** Is it malicious? Can you tell? Have they breached our firewalls?
>
> **Cyber Tech:** Not that we can tell. Should we harden our security temporarily? No network traffic will be able to leave our LAN. Includes emails, internet access, and our public websites.
>
> **Kerr:** What about communications to the moon colony?
>
> **Cyber Tech:** Those channels are encrypted through our satellite system and require authentication to open.
>
> **Kerr:** Yes, then make it so, but leave those communication channels open. Report back if things change or escalate.
>
> **Cyber Tech:** Yes, sir.

They'd come too far to have their plan thwarted by the US government. He wasn't sure why they were suddenly poking around. It slightly concerned him. He knew not to take chances with them or chalk things up to coincidence. He wondered if they had found out about his conversation with King Abdulla? He poured himself a finger of scotch to ease his nerves. "The pressure always intensifies in the eleventh hour," his father used to tell him. "Steel your spine and march forward to grab victory." He swirled the amber liquid around in his crystal tumbler and then threw it back.

"I'm grabbing victory, Father." Dr. Kerr said to himself.

****

The sun was just over the horizon. It was thirty minutes before launch. The air was frigid, and the wind was whipping off the lake. Mel fastened the last Velcro strap on her lunar flight suit. It was tight like a full-body leotard. The material was made from stretchy Nomex, making it fire retardant, in the event of an explosion, she assumed. She swallowed hard, praying she wasn't going to need it for that. She was very anxious. Usually an adventure made her giddy. But this one seemed out of this world. Pun intended. This had her nerves on edge and her stomach in knots. She wondered if this was a mistake? There was a soft knock at the door.

Mel cleared her throat. "Come in," she answered.

Scott stuck his head in. "No one's decent, I hope?" he said in hopes of injecting a little humor into the room. Mel forced a slight smile. He could sense her nervousness right away.

He entered and shut the door. He approached her slowly. He didn't say anything, just looked into those brilliant green eyes.

"Are we going to make it through this?" she finally croaked.

"Are you kidding? Damn right, we are. I already have non-refundable reservations for our celebratory dinner." He smiled that easy smile that drew Mel to him the first time they met, and now she smiled genuinely.

"I'm sorry if I've been a bit bitchy since seeing you in Mexico," she said, casting her eyes down, feeling the heat in her cheeks.

"Awe, nothing to worry about. This whole situation is unbelievably crazy. We all are on edge," he said and tipped her chin up. Her eyes were moist and vulnerable.

"Besides, I was being a brute. I guess I thought I could impress you because I wanted your attention. But you actually impressed me," he said softly.

"I did?"

"Yes. Now show me that fire. Show me the Mel who doesn't give. Let's put a choke hold on this apocalypse and kick its ass."

Mel laughed and said with fresh determination, "Yes, I need to hand out an ass whooping!"

Their eyes held each other's gaze. Then the door burst open, and Scooter stumbled in, cussing and pulling at the Velcro straps of his suit, clearly struggling with it.

"Damn, this thang's binding. I feel like I am walkin' 'round showing everybody my religion!" he said, grunting to get the chest piece secured.

"Let me help you," Mel said, giggling.

"You do look like an overgrown toddler in a onesie," she jested as she fixed his straps, securing him in snuggly.

"Britches are so damn tight. If I fart, I'll blow my boots off!"

"Let's hope not to witness that." Scott scrunched up his nose. The three laughed, then became somber.

"You chillens ready for dis?" Scooter said with a straight face.

"Ready as I am gonna get," replied Scott.

Mel hesitated, then hardened her eyes.

"I was born ready," she said.

"Aight then, it's time to put the chairs in the wagon," replied Scooter. With that, they filed out of the barracks heading to the idling SUV to take them to the launch pad.

****

Masters paced the room holding his cell phone on speaker with Scott on the other line. Scott had his phone on speaker, too, and all three listened intently as the SUV sped toward the launchpad.

"We have a suspect for who might be behind the Chow company's shenanigans. We need to get into the

Planet's Keepers network and snoop around. Usually I rely on you for this, Scott," Masters explained.

"Yeah, well, I think I am booked for the rest of the day. But I gotta guy who can help you. His name's Sully. He tends to be a bit cryptic, but don't let that bother you. He is a bit socially challenged. But he's better than me at infiltrating networks anyway. I'll text him now and connect you both."

"Thank you. I will be patched into communications here in Washington with the Russian Central Command so Sheltie, Master Rob, and myself can monitor things."

"Mel?" It was Rob. He stood next to Masters and spoke into his phone. He needed to hear her voice.

"Right here, big bro," she responded.

"Love you, Sis. Please be careful."

"Will do. And I love you too, big bro. See you on the flip side," she replied softly.

The call ended, and Rob turned and slowly sat down. He could hear the worry in her voice. Dr. Sheltie walked over and put her arms around his neck and hugged him.

"She's gonna be fine. That girl has been through so many rough and tough situations. She'll make it through this one too. You'll see," she whispered in his ear. In her heart she hoped she believed that, too, and gave him a light kiss on the cheek. Then she stood and walked back to her seat and tried to resume her research, but struggled to focus. Not too long ago she was accosted at her office in downtown Dallas by a young man desperately in need of her help. His brain was awash in nightmares, and he hadn't slept in many weeks. She recalled the delirium on his face. She saw the desperation in his eyes. When she learned his name was Rob Florchett, she was stunned. Thankfully, she was able to cure his nightmares, allowing him peaceful rest.

He and his sister's lives were upended many years before when his father was institutionalized and their mother dumped them with a neighbor, never to return. They bounced from foster home to foster home until Mel, then sixteen, ran away from the clutches of a perverted foster dad, but not before she gave him a searing gift. She was never heard from until Rob was able to reunite with her a little more than a week ago after many years apart. Since then, Dr. Sheltie battled with a secret about the siblings and wondered if now was the right time to tell them, with Mel bravely flying into a very dangerous situation. She had hoped there would be a more appropriate time, but things were moving so fast, and now Mel would literally be worlds apart.

Masters's phone rang, interrupting her thoughts and the silence.

"Masters," he answered.

"Hello. This is Sully," the voice replied. It was soft-spoken and secretive. "Scott asked me to give you a call about helping you?"

"Yes, I understand you may be useful in infiltrating a secure network to gather certain intelligence?"

"I may or may not have experience in this, yes."

"What do you need from me?" Masters asked.

"Just your Agency secure call sign for your verification. Then who we may or may not be infiltrating this evening."

Masters recited his secure information. Sully verified it.

"Welcome back, Agent Masters. I'm glad to see our paths have finally crossed."

"Thank you," Masters replied, unsure if what Sully said was a good or bad thing. He recalled Scott explaining his cryptic nature and began to understand what he was referring to.

They discussed the situation with the Planet's Keepers, Dr. Kerr, Chow, ERA, and many other interesting things.

"Give me a few minutes to dig into this and get back to you," Sully said conspiratorially. Then the line went dead.

The conference phone began buzzing. Masters answered it. It was the Russian Central Control patching them into the communications. It relayed that the three passengers were strapped in and ready to begin the preflight checklist. Rob's chest tightened, listening to Scooter run through the prerequisites. Dr. Sheltie looked over and furrowed her brow in concern. Masters stood with his arms crossed, staring at the conference phone and listening intently.

"Ten minutes to lift off," the Central Control voice said in accented English.

Chapter Eighteen

Rodnell Cook separated the Viper from the landing dock. All systems were working perfectly. As the ship eased away from the moon colony, he was debating what he wanted to do first. He recalled a few years back, while the colony was being constructed, he was tasked with finding the gamma-ray device and flashing its firmware with updated code developed by his development team. It would change the operating parameters to implement short bursts of radiation every few minutes, indefinitely, once the main burst was administered during the supermoon moving into a closer orbit with Earth. It was a tricky task because it didn't have the capacitors to sustain more than an initial lengthy burst. It was all it was designed to do. So Cook had to install several upgraded components, which took a couple trips to and from the colony construction site. He wasn't in the Viper back then and recalled the course he took through several low valleys and finally a lengthy canyon that twisted and turned in a way that made him wish he was in the Viper. He decided he would hit that route this trip, but toward the end. He wanted to take the Viper well above the moon's surface and test some of the weaponry systems, see what actually worked and what didn't. Much of the systems were built on theory and tested with Solomon. But the Solomon test environment wasn't even close to really being in space. No simulations on Earth could match all the unfamiliar variables of space travel.

He accelerated upward and began readying the M134 Minigun. This particular flavor of minigun fired 7.62x51 NATO rounds. It featured a Gatling-style rotating barrel assembly run by an electric motor. On Earth it tested perfectly with surprising accuracy. Cook and his team also placed it in an oxygen-free vacuum that simulated space . . . and it worked. Fires can't burn in space, but guns can shoot. Cook's team had manufactured their own ammunition with an oxidizer, a chemical that would trigger the explosion of gunpowder, no atmospheric oxygen required. The only thing to be aware of, like on Earth, was how far the bullet would travel, in case you missed your target. But unlike on Earth, the bullet fired in space will travel quite literally forever because the universe is expanding faster than the bullet can catch up with. This fact is crazy to comprehend, which is why Cook was fascinated to test it.

Once he felt clear of the moon's gravitational pull he readied the weapon. He stalled until the Viper was just floating at a stand-still. Without a target to shoot, he just aimed into the black abyss and pulled the trigger. At first he wasn't sure anything had happened. There was no report to hear from the bullets firing, because there is no sound in space. He did feel a slight thrumming through the cabin of the ship. Then a sphere of powder smoke appeared in front of the ship. It didn't blow away like on Earth, so it became difficult to see through it. He figured he would be moving anyways, not sitting completely still if he was firing at a hostile. So he probably would outrun the plume to keep visibility on his target. He kept this in mind. Also he noticed that Newton's third law of physics occurred. For every action, there is an equal and opposite reaction . . . The Viper actually had started drifting backward from the recoil. Another reason he would need to keep rear thrusters engaged, to counter the gun recoil as the deluge of bullets streamed forward.

He continued his testing at different speeds and noted the changing as the minigun fired. After several test runs, he realized he had almost spent all of his ammunition, so he decided to switch weapon systems to the solid propulsion missiles. For the same reasons the minigun bullets would fire in space, the solid propulsion missiles would too. They, too, contained an oxidizer that didn't require atmospheric oxygen. Also, solid propulsion missiles were more stable and had a much longer shelf life than their liquid-propulsion counterparts. With the minigun, he wanted to test the experience of shooting it in space and was pleased with the outcome. With the missile system, however, he wanted to see the scope of damage. He had made his way quite a distance from the moon colony and felt confident that if he fired into the surface of the moon it would be safe. He brought the Viper closer to the surface and cruised around until he found a mountainous rise ahead that formed a cliff's face. Knowing what he knew now of Newton's third law and its effect using the minigun, he decided to apply the rear thrusters a touch. The HUD was working perfectly, and he sighted in the rocky rise ahead.

Then he fired.

He felt a harsher vibration through the Viper's cabin. The plume of smoke was much more pronounced. The rocket left a perfect cylindrical tunnel behind the missile, unlike anything he had ever seen before. Because he was moving forward when the missile fired, the craft cut through the launch plume, and Cook could easily follow the smoke trail and then the impact against the cliff. At this point he felt he may have made a huge mistake by firing at the surface of the moon. The explosion was strange. There was what appeared to be a flash, but because of the absence of oxygen, it was just a fraction of a second flicker. The top half of the cliff exploded, sending chunks of rocks flying in all directions, including his own. The moon's gravity is a sixth of the earth's, so the exploded objects blew into a starburst pattern and didn't lose speed or trajectory. Within seconds he felt the peppering of pebbles slamming into the outer skin of the Viper. Chinks in his windscreen appeared in his vision, but thankfully didn't penetrate completely. It only took a second to realize the danger he was in, and he quickly increased thrusters and swung the Viper around in the opposite direction, then slammed down the gas. The Viper accelerated instantly as if shot by a catapult. Cook kept close to the moon's surface, hoping its natural curve would keep any further shrapnel above him. After a short time he slowed the craft and took a breath. He had to be more careful. He inspected the chinks in the windscreen and determined its integrity was still solid. As he did a visual inspection out his windows, and he noticed on the right side flank there was a tear in Viper's skin the size of a baseball. The whole exterior of the Viper was coated in a lightweight protective ceramic material called Z93. This is the same coating used to protect the International Space Station. Under the Z93 coating was a thin layer of gold. Gold protects well against corrosion from ultraviolet light and X-rays. Under these two coatings, the main fuselage itself was made of 300-series stainless steel.

Cook wasn't sure whether the hole was something to worry about. He'd have to fly back to the colony where he could appropriately inspect it. Also, he could top off Viper's hydrogen tank for the trip back to Earth. Ahead he saw the entrance to the canyon leading to the area where the gamma-ray device was located. Since it was now on his way back to the colony, he figured he would cruise by it, but not like he first wanted to, at great speed. He needed to update Dr. Kerr about the ship's damage. He figured he would do that now while he headed toward the gamma device. Dr. Kerr wouldn't be happy that Cook may have to delay his return and may choose to start the loading of the passengers before Cook returned. He felt he needed to be there to oversee it all. Cook opened the communication channel for Dr. Kerr, dreading the conversation to come.

****

The takeoff turned out to be thrilling for Mel. The first couple minutes were nerve-wracking, but then her anxiety turned to excitement. Scooter was checking gauges and reporting flight data every few minutes. He was extremely focused but calm. Scott sat back in his seat with his eyes tightly closed, clearly working to maintain even breaths. She felt bad for him. He disliked flying, and this was a flight like no other. She hoped he didn't get sick.

"Regal 3 to John Wayne," the radio crackled.

"John Wayne, copy," said Scooter

"You've exited the earth's atmosphere and are just minutes from the second rocket separation. After that, things will quiet down, and it should be an easy cruise to your destination. Everything appears to be operating under normal parameters," Nakita informed him.

"Well, that just dills my pickle," Scooter replied with clear trepidation in his voice.

"You'll be fine. Let the autopilot take over, and you'll be to the moon in no time."

He wasn't looking forward to this leg of the journey, considering the challenges he had learning to drive craft in the simulator. Hopefully, as Nakita assured, the autopilot would do most of the heavy lifting from here on out. Scooter wouldn't have to do any manual flying, which he dreaded. Flying this spacecraft was nothing like terrestrial craft on Earth. He realized fighting gravity and riding the wind was his preference.

There was a loud clicking sound, then the ride smoothed out considerably. Scooter took a deep breath.

It felt like the moment during take-off where an airplane lifts off the runway.

"Second rocket separation successful," Scooter breathed. Their speed increased dramatically. However, the only way anyone would have known was by watching the speed gauge rolling faster and faster. There were no g-forces or wind noise, just eerie silence and the occasional sound of a beep here and there reporting various milestones of the flight. Scott slowly opened one eye, then the other.

"Why is it so quiet? Are we dead?" he whispered.

"Nope, we still above the worms," Scooter drawled, busy flipping switches and punching buttons.

"Look, it's so beautiful!" Mel screeched, pointing out the window. In the distance was the entire earth framed against a black and star sparkling background.

"Whoa," breathed Scott, his eyes wide. He had seen pictures like this, but seeing it firsthand was breathtaking.

"Well butter my butt and call me a biscuit," Scooter said slowly, just above a whisper. For several minutes they stared in silence as the only world they knew receded into the distance.

****

Masters entered the outer room of the Oval Office. Just minutes earlier he received a text from Lett's assistant that his presence was required immediately by the director. The assistant was waiting by the Oval Office door and jumped up upon his arrival, then ushered him into the room. A handful of people sat around on sofas and chairs, with more in attendance remotely on LCDs hung along a wall. The president stood and offered Masters a seat. Quick introductions from the head of the FBI, Homeland Security, and other top leaders were given. Trey Lett was present too. Masters's stomach tightened. There is no way these people being in the same room was a good sign, especially gathered in this particular office.

"Thank you for joining us on short notice, Ben," the president said as he retook his seat.

"No problem, sir. What's going on?"

"You're aware of the nuclear threat by that Muslim cleric on the news the other evening?"

"Of course, but I also read that the situation may be standing down."

"Thankfully, on a global scale, it is. However, here at home someone didn't get the memo." He then turned to the Homeland Security director. "Tyler, please elaborate on that point for Agent Masters," the president directed. Tyler was a reedy fellow. His suit hung off his limbs like a scarecrow. His hair was thin and combed over to compensate for his balding pate. He wore thick-rimmed glasses, which Masters suspected was to give off the appearance of higher intellect. He could tell the man was a career bureaucrat. The Department of Homeland Security was very new compared to the rest of Washington's alphabet soup. He knew they didn't have the generational experience in their field agents, and their appointed political leaders turned over often. He now realized he was the only field agent in the room. His stomach tightened further.

"We believe through our intelligence reports that a radical Islamic sleeper cell has been activated in the US. We have some specifics, but much is still very fluid," the bureaucrat explained.

"Start with what we know," prompted the president.

"Yes, sir," the bureaucrat said as he stood and handed each person a dossier with Top Secret emblazoned across the top in bright red. "Those joining remotely, you'll find a digital copy of this in your encrypted email." The bureaucrat seated himself, opened his copy, and waited for everyone's attention.

"You're looking at Dr. Heshiek Nizah, a forty-four-year-old American of Middle Eastern descent. He was born in New Jersey and graduated from medical school in 2008. He worked as a board-certified physician for just over seventeen years, gaining several accolades and awards for his work. But don't let his affable smile and seemingly successful career fool you. He was abruptly fired three years ago while serving as a medical director for a large hospital chain."

"Fired for what?" a dark-haired woman on one of the LCD displays asked.

"It seems he couldn't keep his hands off the female staff and apparently was quite socially obnoxious. He had numerous sexual harassment complaints and one lawsuit, which he beat." The bureaucrat paused to turn a few pages in his folder, then continued, "As you can see on page 24, the list of disciplinary actions over his career is long. He filed twelve restraining orders against multiple pissed-off spouses that I assume found out about their wives' involvement with him. Also included here are the court transcripts from his harassment suit. Highlighted are the sections where he took the stand in his own defense, claiming he was the victim. But throughout all of this, the hospital leadership just kept slapping his wrist in favor of the top-quality work he was doing. Apparently his patients loved him, and that was more important. However, in the community, he had built quite a reputation as a womanizer and a drunk. Then the hospital was sold and the new executives implemented new, more strict standards of professional conduct, both at work and otherwise. Soon after, they learned of Nizah being detained by local police for drunken disorderly conduct at a golfing fundraiser. The hospital put him on paid leave while their attorneys sorted out the matter. Ultimately, of course, he wasn't charged and was allowed to resume working with a written reprimand. But not a week back on the job, he was walked in on during a dalliance with a pharmaceutical rep in his office. He was terminated immediately and reported to the state medical board, where his medical license was suspended pending their own investigation. If you read further, you will see that their investigation revealed many other secrets about his proclivities, and his license was subsequently revoked."

"How did he get on your radar?" the president asked.

"Through a missing person's report, filed by his wife of all people, with local law enforcement. They ran a search on his passport and saw it was used the week prior for boarding a plane to Egypt. They searched his personal belongings in his home and office and discovered several correspondences with known terrorist operatives in texts and in an email account he configured on various secret cell phones in his work locker. They were also used to arrange encounters with women and corroborated many of the prior accusations against him. Homeland Security was contacted at that point. We obtained a warrant to wiretap the mosque the group he was contacting frequented as a meeting place. That was two years ago. Then this morning we heard chatter that Nizah is back in the US, but under an alias, which is why we didn't bag him at the airport whenever he returned."

"So why does this bring us here today?" the president asked, irritated that the bureaucrat wasn't getting to the point quick enough.

"Our power grid network was compromised by hackers in the Middle East two days ago. Seems they waltzed right in the front door of it using a vendor's credentials."

"Are you saying they were *given* access?" the director of the FBI said, flabbergasted.

"Or they stole it. We don't know exactly, but we do know certain information was accessed about vulnerable points in each of the three main power grid interconnections. Something terrorists would be very interested in. We also have reason to believe Nizah is working with that knowledge to plan a terrorist attack. Potentially with a dirty bomb." A hush fell over the room as each person considered the implications. A dirty bomb isn't a nuclear device per se. It is a very simple bomb of dynamite, fertilizer, or some other conventional explosive. The kicker is these bombs contain hazardous or radioactive waste materials. The explosion vaporizes the payload to scatter it in the wind. The fallout range varies based on the size of the explosion and weather conditions. A medium-size blast could contaminate up to a one hundred-mile radius if the wind was right on a high-pressure day.

"And how do you know that?" asked the president.

"Several fifty-five-gallon steel drums full of biohazard waste were stolen from a waste disposal building outside of Dallas, Texas. Seems their security is very short-staffed due to the animal uprising. No one wants to leave the building to make the rounds, so it wouldn't be hard for someone to grab a few."

"What a sec. Let's step back for a moment," the dark-haired lady on the LCD screen said. "If the hackers, as you call them, just simply logged into the national grid system using a vendor's credentials, we should know who that vendor is and possibly more information about the trespasser, right?"

"Absolutely. We are already working that angle," the bureaucrat answered smugly, finally appearing slightly competent.

"Well? What vendor is it?" Trey Lett demanded, also becoming flustered with the bureaucrat's lengthy delivery.

"Greener Engineering, owned by none other than Dr. Warwick Kerr, head of the Planet's Keepers."

Instantly the room became abuzz with murmurs and disbelief. Masters glanced at Lett, and they exchanged frowns. He then raised his hands to quiet the room.

"Excuse me . . . Excuse me," he said as the room's attention turned toward him. "May I ask what is my role in this meeting? I'm not a department head of any kind. Just a field operative."

"Of course!" the president exclaimed. He exchanged a look with Trey Lett, then looked back at Masters and said, "With your deep experience in CIA field operations, especially your knowledge and contacts of the terrorist ilk, you've been chosen to track down this Nizah bastard and stop him before he detonates that bomb."

****

Dr. Heshiek Nizah stood in the shadows of a copse of fir trees just north of Dallas, Texas. In front of him on a motorized tripod was a Sony Cyber-Shot RX10 superzoom HD camera. Using an iPad via a Bluetooth connection, Nizah was directing the camera on points of interest, such as the ingress and egress of the North American Electric Co-op campus, recording videos and snapping photos. It wasn't as large a campus as one would imagine for one of the most critical interconnections of the US electric grid. However, it was where his intel sources told him the weakest link in the US electric grid was, because of lack of redundant systems and, recently, lack of security. The stepping down of electricity from the transmission grid to the distribution grid took place in the area in front of him. The transmission grid was where the power was created, and this handoff point was where it started the distribution of that power to hundreds of millions of American homes, businesses, and hospitals, but most importantly, many large municipal water supply systems. It all ran through this facility with no fail-over location to kick in if the facility went offline, and with the world in chaos over the so-called animal apocalypse, this key complex was mostly unguarded. If it was Allah's will, once this facility became disabled, Nizah's true believer brethren would take steps to poison several large water distribution facilities in key places around the country.

His success the next morning was going to be critical to advancing that greater plan.

Only a crazy fool would be tromping about the woods right now with the beasts of the earth on a murderous rampage. But Nizah knew Allah was protecting him. This was a divine mission that he wouldn't fail. How did he know this? Like many Muslims, Nizah was seduced by the ways of the Great Western Satan, the so-called American Dream. He found himself tempted for years by uncountable wicked Jezebels that roamed the halls of the hospitals and clinics he had worked in. They were easily enamored by his physician stature and wealth, making his carnal conquests quite easy. With his large income, excesses of every kind were easily obtained, and he quickly lost his spiritual way because of it. But now, he stood here sober and repentant. Two years ago, he left his unclean family and flew to Egypt to perform a secret pilgrimage to Mecca in hopes of restoring his faith. Once there, taken in by the highest clerics of Islam, he maintained a simple life of studying the Koran and daily prayer to cleanse and purify his soul from the opulent ways of the West.

Then just days ago the opportunity for the penance of his past sins manifested before him. The clerics explained that the Prophet Muhammad himself had provided them with very detailed and intimate knowledge of this weakness in the US grid. They envisioned it would potentially save millions of Allah's true believers from a worldwide nuclear catastrophe. When hearing this, Nizah believed in his heart that Allah *must* have ordained it. He eagerly volunteered for this mission to begin atonement and thus was assigned to the cell of Muslim warriors local to this grid facility. He couldn't wait to play his role. No, he wouldn't fail. The plan was very straightforward, and every detail he needed to execute it successfully was on his iPad. Allah watches over his own. Praise be to him.

****

Special Agent Benjamin Masters stood in front of Dr. Sheltie and Rob back in the secure meeting room. He explained what had transpired in the Oval Office with the president, Trey Lett, and others.

"But why you? Why not local law enforcement in Dallas. They should have plenty of federal and local resources," Dr. Sheltie asked, puzzled about why Masters should assume this risk and responsibility.

"On any normal day they would. However, it seems with this apocalypse occurring, law enforcement is absent, doesn't exist right now," Masters explained.

"That's absurd. How can law enforcement just not exist?" Dr. Sheltie retorted, clearly upset with this decision.

"It just doesn't. Let's keep focus. This Dr. Nizah, we think, is targeting the North American Electric Co-op's interconnection site. Here is why we think this based on the intelligence we are gathering." Masters laid down a schematic showing where the transmission grid and the distribution grid came together.

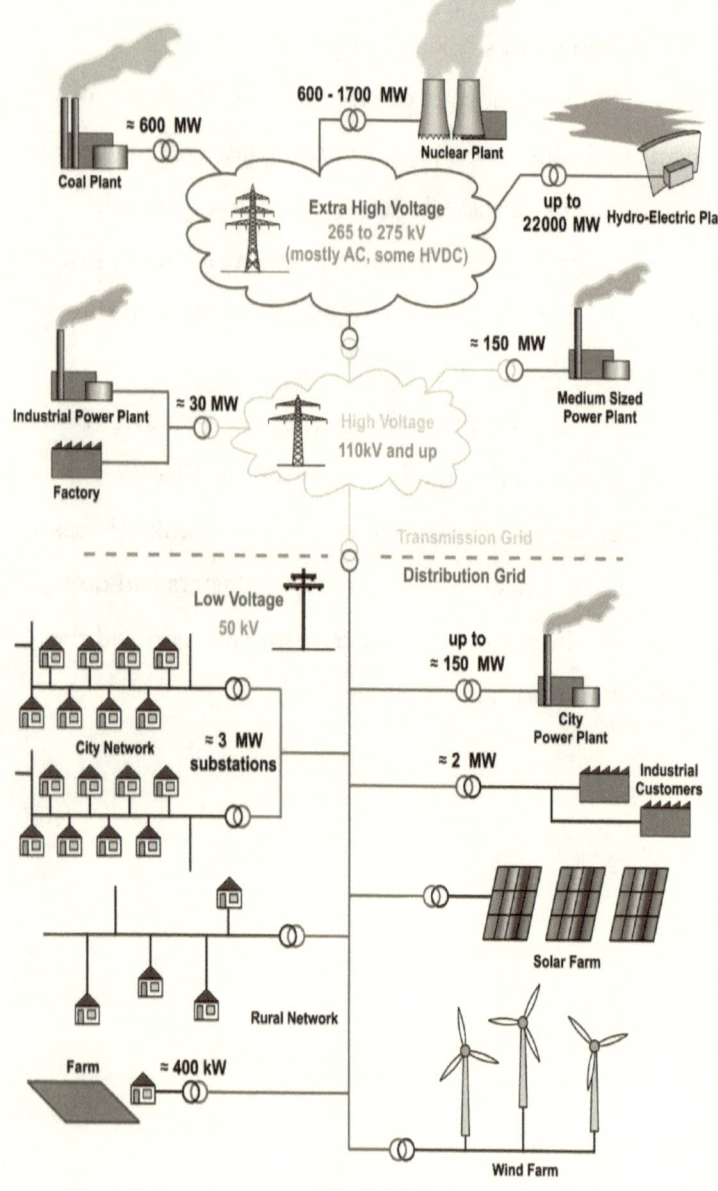

He tapped the two circles that overlapped in the center of the drawing that represented this point.

"The facility is outside of a small community called Prosper, Texas. I'm catching a charter jet there in a few minutes."

"What about us? We can help you," Rob said, but Masters shook his head.

"At least we know now that Dr. Kerr is the mastermind behind all of this, even tied to this terrorist threat. We must find him before another shoe drops. I need you both to stay here and see if you can find Dr. Kerr's location," Masters explained. As if on cue, his cell phone rang.

"It's Sully," he announced, seeing the number. "Masters here."

"Hey there. I hope you're sitting down, 'cause this is some crazy shit," Sully said urgently.

"What did you find?"

"They caught me poking around in their DMZ and hardened their firewalls. That alone told me I was dealing with a heavy security presence, 'cause I never get my IP pinned like that. They were on me right away."

"Bear in mind I know nothing of what you are talking about. DMZs, firewalls, IPs . . . You gotta dumb it down for me," Masters interrupted. It seemed brainiacs, no matter what variety, always talked in their own language.

"It doesn't matter. That's not important right now. Anyways, I noticed they had an encrypted satellite uplink. Man, they are using AES 512 encryption. That algorithm isn't available for public release yet. So this setup isn't for cell phones and stuff average companies may use it for, no way. What we're talkin' about here is equipment for talking to entities in outer space. Like NASA shit. So immediately, I got to thinking, what does an environmental group need with such a thing, right?" Sully was speaking more rapidly and at a higher pitch as his excitement began to peak. Masters sensed his news was going to be something big. He didn't take Sully as the excitable type.

Sully continued, "So the firewall ports they use for sat comms were shut during the hardening process. However, they must be configured to open upon a credentialed handshake request."

"Sully, you're losing me again," Masters warned, rubbing his temples.

"Just stay with me, man. I gotta a lot of ground to cover here, so just understand what you can and then ask questions when I finish. Cool?"

"Um, OK . . . cool."

"OK, well at that exact moment luck struck 'cause the sat comm ports opened up out of nowhere. I'm guessing a call request came through. I obviously couldn't sniff it 'cause it was too heavily encrypted, but it did open a door for me to breach their security and ghost myself so they couldn't detect me. These guys are good. Not to brag too much, but I'm way damn better."

"I have no doubt. Let's move this forward to the lead of the story." Masters could hear Sully smiling with pride through the phone. He didn't want to downplay the guy's talent, but time was of the essence. For the next several minutes Sully filled them in on everything he found. All three listening were stunned beyond belief.

"So you're telling us that you have *proof* that the Planet's Keepers purposely created this animal apocalypse by exploiting the genetically modified feed through the Chow company to kill any and all human life in order to restore the planet back to what they are calling Eden? And further, they have built a sustainable moon colony and the means to populate it with Dr. Kerr's chosen people?" Masters could hardly believe what he was saying.

"Yes, siree. And don't forget I found schematics for a pretty wicked spacecraft they call the Viper, rigged out with modern fighter jet–style weaponry! Annnnd . . . per the travel logs I hacked, it appears to be up there right now!" Sully said with emphasis.

"Oh no. Mel." Rob groaned, feeling suddenly sick. If this was true, then Scooter, Scott, and Mel could be in grave danger.

The conference phone came to life with Scooter doing his top-of-the-hour check-in with the Russian control center.

"John Wayne to control, do ya read?"

"Control, copy."

"We 'bout two hours from tator pickin' time. Everything looks normal on our end. Systems are purring along like a kitty in a milk factory. Our two cosmonauts are preppin' their gear to walk da chalk when we arrive."

There was a pause as the Russian control team had to Google search all of Scooter's Southern quips.

"OK, John Wayne, roger that."

"Kinda likin' it up here. So peaceful and calm," Scooter intoned over the phone.

"I sure hope it stays that way," Rob muttered. Dr. Sheltie reached over and squeezed his arm to comfort him. Her own anxiety was spiking as well.

Chapter Nineteen

Rodnell Cook clicked off the secure call with Dr. Kerr. To say Dr. Kerr was unhappy about Cook's delay was putting it mildly. He was livid. Kerr demanded Cook return to the moon colony to assess and repair any damage to the Viper and then return to Earth immediately so they could start launching the pods. Cook had never been dressed down so vehemently in his life. Yes, it was stupid to fire a missile at that cliff, but to be demeaned and insulted for it, that infuriated him. Cook was glad the decision to start the pod launching process without him didn't come up because seeds of doubt about this whole plan were creeping into his mind. He aborted his route to the gamma-ray device and plotted a course to the colony. He would have to park it in one of the loading bays that had an air lock. This way he could work on the damage without having to put on a space suit. It would take a bit longer to situate everything, but it should save time in the long run by not having to fumble around inside a space suit. Repairs were usually tedious, and wearing the oversized gloves of the suit would just make things more difficult.

Ahead he saw the glow of the moon colony. He docked the ship and went inside to ready the loading bay for the Viper's entrance. Now he felt uneasy, unsure about this whole mission. Yes, he had achieved amazing feats in technology with his programming and engineering teams. There was no doubt about that. Just walking through the halls of this structure situated on the dark side of the moon, of all places, was a testament to that. What was bugging him was the fact it wasn't done to further mankind. It was done to preserve just a few. Cook wouldn't get the recognition he deserved. Not that recognition was a priority for him, but what came next? If this were an international effort by multiple countries coming together to further human survival, then there would always be challenges to overcome, reasons to push further. With Dr. Kerr and the Planet's Keepers, he doubted much more up here would be pursued further. Even if this crazy animal frenzy succeeded, Kerr and his disciples would return to Earth. Cook wanted to continue engineering in space, not reconstructing or repairing old technology on Earth for just a few environmental lunatics.

The environment was never his motivation in this scheme, ever. It was always the challenge to push limits and create the impossible. The Planet's Keepers gave him that stage to work on. But now, Cook wondered if it was the wrong stage. He hated with every fiber of his being his government and those responsible for the death of his wife and baby son. But did he hate all mankind? There was a moment he probably did, but now he did not. There still existed good people working toward a greater good for all humanity. Evil was always present and came in different forms, he had no doubt about that. There always needed to be a good force fighting the evil forces to balance the scales. In his heart, he didn't consider Dr. Kerr and the Planet's Keepers to be a good force. How he got caught up in this radical cult to this point, he didn't know. He should have realized this before. He decided then and there he would consider disabling the gamma-ray device himself. In his mind he wasn't sure if he could commit to it just yet, but he needed to look at it one more time. At that point, he would commit himself to either saving humanity or saving the planet.

****

Masters landed at a small private airport in McKinney, Texas. With no one around, it didn't take long for him to find a suitable vehicle to drive north toward the small community of Prosper, Texas. On the way, he needed to make a stop at a prominent Muslim mosque. Dawn was quickly approaching, and he knew time was short. Maybe even too short. At any moment he expected to hear a boom and see a mushroom cloud in the distance. Even as such, the stop at the Mosque was necessary. He hoped he didn't have to drag his contact out, but he would if he had to. There was very little activity as people still surviving were locked away from the evolutionary killing machines. He had seen a few beasts moving around in shadows, making him feel uneasy. He kept his speed up to avoid a confrontation with them if he could help it. Beside him was a shoulder tote full of tools, maps, and bullets for his Glock holstered under his jacket. He wasn't sure what to expect in the way of the dirty bomb if it came to it that he had to disarm it. He did have bomb squad–style training, but it had been several years back. No intel was gathered about the bomb's makeup or size. Just that multiple fifty-five-gallon steel drums of the biohazard sludge were stolen. He felt if he didn't stop Nizah before it was set, then it would be too late to disarm it anyways, especially if he had ambitions of martyrdom and was rewarded by Allah his own planet of virgins. Knowing what he knew about Nizah and his perversions, a planet full of virgins probably did sound pretty good to him.

Masters could now see the mosque's huge illuminated golden domes in the distance. He pulled over and made sure no animal abominations were lurking about. Seeing he was alone, he took out his cell and punched in a number. If his contact didn't answer, then he would have to force his way in and find him. Thankfully it was answered. He hoped for some new information to fill in some blanks about Nizah's plan.

"Yes," a man answered in Arabic.

"Malik, your food is ready." There was silence for a beat or two. Masters thought Malik had disconnected.

Then a hushed voice in accented English said, "How spicy is it?"

"Extremely."

"Do I pick it up, or can you deliver it?"

"Delivery is not an option."

The man on the phone sighed deeply.

"Which restaurant?"

"The one on Rainbow Road," Masters answered.

"I am not far," Malik replied and the line did disconnect.

Masters had met Omar Malikallah several years before while on assignment in the Middle East. "Malik" was what Masters came to call him over the years. He was one of a very few CIA assets deep within radical Islam. So deep that Malik would not acknowledge any outsider except Masters. And even with Masters, he always held back from doing anything more than providing information. He was a true believer in Islam as a peaceful religion and vehemently disagreed with its radical wing. However, confronting the radicals directly was guaranteed death. He found healthier results by passing as a Muslim cleric and eavesdropping on meetings and conversations. He would then leak that to Masters so the CIA could interfere with the radical groups' plans. Masters knew Malik would be here in Dallas because he followed all the holy warriors around, blessing their souls for Allah before martyrdom.

They developed a code language around food. The spicier the dish, the more urgent the request. If it was to be delivered, it meant Masters had sent information through their prearranged channels. If delivery wasn't an option, then Masters was requesting an in-person meeting. To identify the meeting place, Masters had assigned certain locations fake street names. Rainbow Road referred to a CIA safehouse close by in Frisco, Texas, just outside of the small community of Prosper, where the North American Electric Co-op campus was located. The fact Malik was physically here answered the question of whether this was a suicide mission or not. Masters knew he had little time. He sped off in the direction of the safe house.

He arrived ten minutes later and pulled into the driveway. The house was a modest one-story like every fourth house on that street. He got out and looked around, ever vigilant for deranged animals that may be nearby. Seeing none, he walked to the garage door keypad and punched the code. The door raised, and he pulled into the left side, leaving the right for Malik. Within minutes a compact Toyota turned into the driveway and parked on the right-hand side. Masters hit the button and the garage door lowered. He then felt the top of the door frame and found a key. He unlocked the door that led into the kitchen and entered the house. The alarm began beeping, and he quickly typed in the disarming code. He pulled his gun and silently began scanning the rooms to ensure the house was empty. Dried specks of vomit were around the sink where Dr. Sheltie had gotten sick at the images she witnessed in Masters's nightmarish dreams. He entered the living room and saw the couch on which he lay as she cured him of them through a unique style of hypnosis. It didn't seem like all of this was just days ago. It felt like years, even a whole lifetime ago with all that had happened since.

He returned to the kitchen to find Malik, dressed like a typical Islamic cleric, standing and looking at him intently.

"I know what you want," Malik said in a serious tone.

"But?" Masters asked.

"You said our arrangement was satisfied back in Afghanistan. Scrutiny of me since Kabul nearly uncovered my involvement in thwarting that attack on the US base. You know I am still being watched closely, yet you insist I come here?" Malik said, becoming agitated.

"I've offered you protection if you want out."

"There is no out, Ben. My family will be killed if I just vanish. The paranoia of the radicals would make them assume I flipped. I've seen this happen time and time again when others have just *vanished*."

"Malik, your family won't survive this apocalypse either if you don't help me."

"The world is ending. Why do I care about terrorist attacks? At least now my family and I have some semblance of safety within the mosque, even if it is for a short time. Allah will protect us if it is His will."

"There is a plan underway to stop the apocalypse."

"Ha! This is ordained by the Prophet Muhammad. Even the mighty United States can't stop it. Don't be a fool."

"Actually, all of this was preordained by a radical environmentalist. The Prophet Allah had nothing to do with it."

Malik just stared at him. He knew Masters was honorable, and if he said this wasn't the true End Times, then Malik believed him. It wouldn't be the first time one religion or another had falsely predicted the end of days. Masters could see the man was battling his faith once again.

Masters continued, "If we stop the apocalypse, then the world will keep going on. We have to stop this terrorist attack. It's still crucial to all people, Muslims and Christians alike. So much senseless death has already happened, then to compound that with disabling the power grid? Makes no sense and does nothing to further Islam as a peaceful religion, which is what you stand for. You've always seen through short-sighted radicalism. Help me here, Malik."

Malik exhaled a breath and rubbed his face.

"If what you say is true, I will help you."

"It's true. You know I don't waste time playing games."

"When this is over, will you guarantee the safety of me *and* my family?"

"Guarantee I cannot. But try, yes. I doubt anyone wouldn't agree to that as grave as this situation is."

Malik took a deep breath. "You may be too late. Nizah has already picked up the truck loaded with the explosives," he said quickly. "He is heading to the north gate of the North American Electric Co-op campus. The gate has been abandoned after several guards were killed by animals two days ago. Since then, any guards that still may be there have refused to man the guard shack at that entrance. He will ram through the gate and proceed to the center of the campus where the step-down turbines that convert the higher voltage to the distribution grid are located. There is a shallow indentation under it with just enough clearance for the truck. He is going to pull into it and then detonate. It will be so quick, no one will be able to stop him."

"What's the payload?" Masters asked urgently.

"Just over ten thousand pounds of francium waste in specialized fifty-five gallon drums wrapped in I don't know how much C4 explosive. I just know it's C4."

Masters was silent a second, making calculations in his head. Francium and C4? "Where the hell did you guys get your hands on francium and C4?" he said, exasperated. Biohazard waste was bad enough, but francium is waste from a nuclear facility and *extremely* radioactive. Why would it be stored at a typical biohazardous waste treatment plant? This was becoming worse by the second. He knew he wouldn't get these answers now and had to move fast. He clapped Malik on the shoulders and said, "Thank you, my friend. Let's hope I'm not too late."

Just before exiting into the garage, he turned and said, "Hey, Malik." Malik turned to look at Masters. "You *are* an honorable man." With that Masters was out the door. He hit the garage door opener on the wall, jumped into his car, and sped off.

"I hope Allah agrees. Praise be," said Malik quietly to himself as he watched Masters squeal away.

****

Ahead, Dr. Nizah could see the North end gate into the North American Electric Co-op campus. He slowed the rental box truck to observe. The guard shack still appeared empty. His adrenaline spiked, and his heart rate accelerated. As a doctor, he knew he had a short time to take advantage of it before he lost his nerve. He tried not to think that within just minutes, his life would be over. He knew it would be instantaneous, without pain. That really didn't comfort him though. But what did he have to live for anyways? He would never practice medicine again. He'd abandoned his family, and they now had moved on. But what really bothered him was to never again feel the soft, warm curves of a woman's body. It had been over two years since he had felt a young nurse bucking around atop him or him driving his insatiable manhood into her soft, warm flesh. Why didn't he indulge himself just once before now? Because. Because he had been focused. And focused he needed to stay. He strained to push these lust-filled thoughts from his head. He had to. Filthy Jezebels. Allah would provide all the womanly pleasures he could ever desire as a martyr. He placed the detonation trigger on his lap.

"I'm doing this. Praise be to Allah!" He gripped the steering wheel with both hands and put the gas pedal to the floor. The truck revved high and sped forward.

The gate was twelve feet high and made of chain-link fencing on a pulley system. Atop was heavily coiled razor wire. Not a single soul in sight. He could see a heavy chain locking the gate tight. He centered the nose of the truck to the middle of the gate and held his grip firmly. Fifty feet from impact. As he approached within a dozen feet, he noticed something across his path just beyond the gate itself. It was too late to stop. The truck plowed through the gate. It folded around the nose of the truck and spiderwebbed the windshield, but the truck barreled through with ease. flinging it violently open. The truck sped forward. Nizah could see the entry to where he was to park and detonate. He turned toward it and realized his steering was becoming less responsive and the truck was becoming sluggish.

"Come on, you piece of shit!" he yelled, slapping the steering wheel. He pressed the gas down further. He could see white smoke billowing behind him. Why was the truck slowing? Something must have happened upon impact with the gate. He was finally forced to stop. He tossed the detonation switch into the passenger seat and climbed out of the truck. The front tires were flat, and the rear tires were shredded and smoking. In his reconnaissance, he had failed to see the row of underground road spikes that were now deployed just inside the gate. He cursed loudly, then turned and looked ahead. He was so close, but he knew he had to be under the turbine shaft to disable it completely.

"Fuck it," he mumbled, and turned to walk back to the open driver's door. He would drive it on its rims if he had to. One way or the other, he was determined to succeed. He grabbed the handle and pulled himself back into the driver's seat. He turned to retrieve the detonation switch and froze in shock. Seated next to him was a man. Masters punched Nizah square in the face, sending him sprawling out of the truck onto the pavement. Masters quickly climbed out of the truck and walked around to Nizah, lying on his back dazed. His nose was smashed into his face and bleeding profusely. Masters pulled his gun and pointed it at him.

"Wait! Wait! I'm a doctor! Please don't shoot me!" Nizah yelled in garbled noises through his crushed face. He was waving his hands in front of him. Masters stood over him, unmoved by his pleading.

"I save lives! Please don't kill me." Nizah was now sniveling, tears pouring from his eyes. What a coward. Putting a bullet in his head was warranted, and he wouldn't lose sleep over it. Masters doubted anyone would miss this sick scum. But he knew that would be a sweet release for this prick, doctor or not.

"Compare that number to how many women you've preyed upon, families you've torn apart, and who knows how many innocent people you would have killed with this bomb? Your savior complex gains no sympathy from me," he said, then aimed and pulled the trigger. The .45-caliber Glock bucked in his hand. The hollow-point bullet caught Nizah square in his crotch, severing his groin and splattering his precious manhood into a bloody ruin. Nizah's eyes widened and rolled back as he balled himself up, silently screaming.

If he bleeds out, it would be a kindness, Masters thought as he walked back around to retrieve the detonation switch from the passenger side. He pocketed it in his jacket and then started back toward his car, parked outside the open gate. He punched Lett's name on his phone.

"Oh God, please tell me you're alive and the bomb is secure. Or at least tell me the bomb is secure," Lett said right away.

"Ha, yeah, the bomb is secure. And for what it's worth, I'm still alive too," Masters replied.

"Good man!" Lett said as a huge cheer erupted in the background. Masters explained the moments from him landing at the airport and speaking with Malik and his promise to the man.

"For sure. Once this animal hell is fixed, we can start arranging him and his family's extraction into a protection program immediately," Lett confirmed. Masters was about halfway to his car when he heard a tap, tap, tapping coming from different directions behind him. He paused and slowly turned around, then froze.

"Masters? Ben, are you there?" Lett asked when Masters failed to answer a question.

"Uh, yeah. I'm here. But . . . I gotta let you go. Something pressing has come up."

Fanned out behind him were five of the largest, most terrifying dogs he had ever seen. It was hard to determine their breed with all the evolutionary growth and deformities they had. His best guess was that in their normal size and shape, some were Doberman pinschers, and some may have been pit bulls. Not that it mattered. He was sure a pack of chihuahuas would be just as lethal right now. In the distance behind the dogs, he could hear Nizah screaming as two other creatures began ripping him apart. *Now that's a shame*, Masters thought sourly. He had hoped that the sick son of a bitch would live a long life without the pleasure of his best little friend. That would be a more fitting dose of justice than death. But what was done was done, as multiple pieces of Nizah were being fought over and dragged away, leaving trails of crimson gore under the array of sodium lights all around.

The tapping noises continued, coming from the beasts' elongated claws scraping on the hard concrete surface. Tap, tap, tap, tap as the beasts positioned themselves around Masters. In the distance there were more beastly shadows lurking that looked to be German shepherd dogs. Others began emerging from behind some machinery. These were bigger than all the rest. Masters could feel the deep growls echoing all around him. No wonder this place was abandoned. It seemed to have turned into the epicenter of this apocalyptic hell.

He slowly slipped his phone into his pocket. Then ever so gently, he pulled his Glock out of its holster and began considering his options. If there were any.

****

Scooter was all concentration as he approached the moon's surface. He flipped up the covers of the landing gear switches and exposed their toggle buttons. He started switching them in the appropriate sequence. This was the only part of the simulator training that he wasn't able to cover as thoroughly as he would have liked. There was only so much time before the launch, and a priority was established on what he was to focus on. The lunar landing was on the lower end of that list. It was supposed to be as simple as holding the ship at a hover, pushing the deployment buttons, and then just like a chopper, easing it down to the surface. But of course one slight detail wouldn't line up.

"John Wayne to control, do you copy?" he drawled.

"We copy you, John Wayne."

"The landin' gear has deployed, but the lockin' light on one of the legs didn't come on. Is this concerning to anyone?" There were four landing legs, each six feet long. Each extended below the craft using hydraulic motors. Once they were fully extended, they would lock into place, causing a light on the control board to light up. One of them was not lighting up.

"Try retracting it, and then deploy again. Maybe there is debris in the sleeve," Control instructed. Scooter complied, but the light still did not illuminate.

"That's a negatory, my good Communist buddy."

"Continue in a holding pattern until further instructions," Control replied.

"Is this bad?" Mel asked. Her visor was open on her space suit. She and Scott were rigged out for their moonwalk.

"Dunno. The leg could actually be locked and the light is just malfunctioning," Scooter answered.

"Or it's not actually locked. Then what?" Scott asked.

"Then we topple over like an acorn calf," Scooter replied as he tried the landing gear one more time with no success.

"John Wayne, this is Regal 3. Do you copy?" asked Nakita.

"Yes, ma'am. I could *copy* you all day long."

Nakita smirked, then said, "We don't know what to do. No one can exit without the craft landing. You're going to have to try to land."

"Ooooh, boy. I knew you was gonna say dat." Scooter flipped a couple more switches and then instructed Mel and Scott to buckle in. After everyone was secure, he said, "Down we go, everybody."

The ship lowered slowly.

"Contact in three . . . two . . . one . . ." Scooter counted off. There was a jolt, and everything seemed fine.

"Nice job, Scooter!" Mel said excitedly. Then they felt the craft begin to list to one side.

"Aww, hell. Brace yourself!" Scooter yelled. The craft jolted hard to one side as the unlocked landing gear retracted and the other locked one on the same side snapped in half under the ship's weight being distributed wrong. In a billow of moon dust, the craft settled.

"Everyone good?" Scooter asked. Mel and Scott said they were fine. But somewhere there was a hissing sound. Suddenly a red alarm light came on and started flashing.

"John Wayne to Regal 3."

"Regal 3, go ahead, John Wayne."

"Our ox just slid in the ditch."

Chapter Twenty

Rodnell Cook climbed down from the top of the Viper. The shrapnel holes in the ship were just superficial. The skin was punctured, but the stainless steel fuselage was not damaged, as he'd hoped. He took some patching adhesive and cut off several strips. He layered them in one direction, then put a second layer in the other direction. Then with a torch, he heated the strips to activate the adhesive compound. Then using a smoothing roller, he made sure it was fully adhered. It didn't take long for the fast-acting epoxy to harden, making the shell solid again.

After the repairs were completed, he walked the entire colony one last time, making sure everything was functional and ready. Ready for what, he didn't know at this point. He suddenly felt melancholy. Somehow he figured this may be the last time he would see it. All around him were memories of all the years of research, testing, and construction to build the first sustainable colony on the moon. What an achievement, and only a couple dozen people might ever know about it—all of them being wealthy narcissists who would never appreciate such a feat. He knew this was the rub. Just yesterday he was brimming with excitement. Funny how things can change so quickly, causing one's mood to change as well. He boarded the Viper and powered it on. All systems looked good. He had topped off the liquid hydrogen tank to ensure plenty of fuel to make it back. But before he turned toward Earth, he wanted to see the gamma-ray device one last time to determine which way he was going to commit. He hated being indecisive. He just knew if he could look at it one more time and then if he left it active, he would be fine with that. If he decided to destroy it, he would be fine with that too. He just needed to decide so there would be no second-guessing himself later. He hit the button to release the air lock, and the loading bay door began lifting up. Once the door was raised completely, he slowly reversed out. Safely outside the loading bay, he closed the door and reactivated the air lock. He then turned the Viper in the direction of the gamma-ray device and accelerated.

****

The alarm light turned solid red on the control board, and an audible beeping began.

"Nakita, what the hell does this alarm mean?" Scooter said, dropping the use of call signs and radio handles altogether.

"You're losing cabin pressure. Something must have punctured the fuselage during the impact," she replied.

"Put your visors down and turn your oxygen on," Scooter said to Mel and Scott. He quickly stood up and walked into the rear section. They helped each other with their oxygen regulators, and Scooter returned with a space suit of his own.

"Help me here," he said to them. They quickly assisted him into it and opened his oxygen regulator. On each of their wrists were buttons that controlled the suits' electronic capabilities. Scooter mimed for them to push the comms button.

"Can you hear me?" he asked them. They nodded affirmatively. He then said, "Breaker, breaker. Can I get a radio check from control?" Scooter asked, reverting to terrestrial CB jargon.

"This is control, we read you loud and clear."

"I'm going out to see what's happened. How much oxygen do we have?"

"Between six and eight hours, depending on your breathing. Try to stay calm and manage your breath to maximize your supply," Nakita explained.

"Let's open the outer hatch," Scooter instructed. They moved into the air lock and popped the hatch. The hatch side of the ship was up in the air, so when it opened, they just saw complete blackness with glittering stars. Scooter pulled himself up easily in the low gravity and peeked out.

"We definitely out past where the buses run. It's blacker than truck stop coffee out here," he said as he worked his way out.

"You next," Scott said to Mel. With their solar shields down, they couldn't see each other's faces, only their own reflection. Scott wondered if he would ever see Mel's beautiful green eyes again. That made him swallow hard. He started to doubt they were going to survive this trip after all. Before he exited, he grabbed the tool bag they'd packed to disable the gamma-ray device. Just because his death was sealed in the next six to eight hours didn't mean the death of those on Earth should be as well. He decided he still was going to complete his part of the mission no matter what.

Scooter was on the surface making his way to where the ship lay on its side. He quickly saw the issue.

"There's our problem," he pointed when Mel and Scott joined him. The back corner of the craft was crinkled inward on a cluster of sharp rocks. Hydraulic and other fluids were spilling out around the rocks. The damage was extensive, and he knew there was no fixing it with the tools and supplies they had on hand. This required custom machining to patch just the hole. Even if he could patch it, he could tell there were internal mechanical repairs needed too.

"Is it serious?" Mel asked.

"As serious as the business end of a twelve-gauge. And turns out probably just as deadly for us too," he said, perplexed. All three stared in silence, thinking about the problem, but more so the ramifications of it.

"Well, I'm gonna go see about bringing the gamma ray device offline. It'll take my mind off all this," Scott said, and turned to go.

"I'll help you," Mel followed.

"I'll keep here and exist. At least for six more hours, anyways," Scooter muttered to himself. He waited until they were far enough away that their comms lost connection. He didn't want them to hear the next conversation. Once he was sure they were out of range, he asked, "Nakita, you there?"

"Yes, Scooter?"

"What's gonna happen?"

"What do you mean?"

"I mean the end. When the oxygen runs out."

"Don't worry about that now. Keep describing what you are seeing, and maybe we can . . ."

"No, galdammit! I need to know. Tell me what happens when the air runs out!" he shouted, interrupting her. There was a long pause. He could hear her struggling to hold it together.

"OK, fine. You really want to know?" she snapped back at him, angry he was making her explain how he would die.

"Yes, ma'am. Please," he said, barely audible.

"You'll lose pressure in your suit and be susceptible to the surface temperature, which I am currently showing to be 248 degrees Fahrenheit. Water boils at a much lower temperature in space, so since your body is roughly 60 percent water, your body tissues will begin to expand rapidly. The air will be sucked out of your lungs. Your instinct will be to hold it, but do not." She felt tears stinging her eyes. She sucked in a ragged breath, then continued, "The air will expand rapidly and burst your lungs. Save yourself the pain and just exhale." A tear slid down her cheek, but she still held it together. "All the oxygen in your blood will dissipate, starving your brain. You'll lose consciousness after about ten or fifteen seconds anyway . . ." Tears flowed more freely now as she squeezed her eyes closed. "And you'll die of hypoxia," she breathed out the last words and wiped the tears from her cheek.

There was a full minute's pause. Then Scooter broke the silence. "I always heard the body don't decompose in space," he said in a light voice. "You just turn into a biggo stick of beef jerky. Is dat true?"

"More or less. You silly cowboy," she whispered with a smile. It was then she realized she loved Scooter, though she'd just known him a few days. No one ever in her whole life made her laugh like he did. From the moment they met on the ferry dock, she knew there was a natural connection between them. Bantering with him about poisoning his vodka to the late nights just talking over bland food and even worse beer were so very special to her now. She longed to hold him, feel his warmth and feel his soft lips against hers. She'd just assumed there would be an opportunity for that stuff later. Now she ached with regret. She wasn't sure she could be there when his oxygen depleted.

****

"I wish you wouldn't have followed me," Scott said curtly as he stalked in the direction of the gamma-ray device. He could see it on a slight rise ahead.

"Scott, wait! Slow down." She grabbed his arm and turned him to her.

"What?" he said testily.

She couldn't figure out why she felt a knot forming in her throat. She couldn't see his face, but imagined the hurt etched into it. They were doomed for death. What could she say to possibly comfort him?

"Look, go help Scooter. I'll take care of this. I need to be alone," he said, and walked away. The truth was he was scared out of his mind and didn't want Mel to see him if he broke down. After exiting the craft and realizing they weren't leaving this God-forsaken rock, his mind started displaying memories of the people he loved, his family, his friends. He would never see them again or be able to tell them goodbye. Hell, now that he thought about it, he never told any of them he was even on this mission. They may never know. His death would probably get swept under a CIA rug in Washington. The truth would be bottled away until one day in the distant future, it formed a leak, spilling the truth. But then no one would mourn him. Too much time would have passed.

He realized he was standing beside the gamma-ray device, but was so lost in thought he was just staring at it. He didn't realize Mel had followed him.

"Hey. You OK?" she said softly. Her voice was the most beautiful sound in the universe to Scott, but he wasn't holding up very well and snapped at her.

"Look! Go away! Let me just disable this stupid thing." He rummaged in the tote for the huge insulated wire cutters. He found them and stalked over to the device. He paused a second, realizing something about it was different from the fake one they had trained on. Instead of a single, thick cable to cut, there were two. Both were identical, and he couldn't tell which one to use the cutters on. Mel saw him hesitating.

"What? What is it?" she said, walking over. Then she saw the double cable conundrum. "There was just supposed to be one cable, right?" she asked.

"Yes," he said, thinking.

"It must be the modifications made to it that allowed the maintenance pulses. And that silver box bolted on the back, there, is new too. Let's go back to the ship so we can talk to control and see what . . ."

"No. I'll cut them both," he said, cutting her off.

"We have time, Scott."

"Time is something we don't have! We'll be dead in less than six hours! Don't you get that!" he yelled back.

Mel stepped back, panicked. She worked to control her breathing like she had learned in her martial arts training, taking control of her emotions.

"Well you can't cut anything until we remove the access panel and unplug the capacitor boards. Remember what we were instructed. You'll blow yourself up if you don't and cut those wires," she advised in as calm a voice as she could muster.

"No, I'm cutting them."

"Scott, NO!" she screamed, but he already had the cutter's jaws open around both wires. She lunged for him, but it was too late. She'd never be able to describe what she saw in the no-oxygen vacuum of the moon's surface. It wasn't really a flash but a strange rippling of the air. Only one cable severed from the cut, and the energy it released kept Scott from applying enough pressure to cut both. The severed one whipped back and lashed his leg above his left knee as the inertia from the energy smacked him back. He skidded on his back several feet.

Mel screamed and rushed to him. She couldn't see his face, and he wasn't moving. Above his left knee, his space suit was torn open. She could see his pressure blowing out and blood droplets splattering about. She instinctively grabbed around his thigh to stop the air leak, but his thighs were too thick for her small hands to completely seal the leak off.

"Scott! Scott!" she yelled, but he just lay there motionless.

"Shit, shit, shit," she cursed under her breath as she struggled to think what to do. Scooter was out of range of her comm unit. At least Scott's oxygen was still flowing. She released his leg and quickly rummaged around in the tool tote.

"No," she grumbled, as nothing in there seemed to be helpful. Ah! Yes! In the bottom was a roll of duct tape, and she grabbed it.

"Thank you, thank you, thank you," she said as she rushed back to his side. Her thick gloves made starting the tape off the roll almost impossible.

"Come on, come on, come on," she breathed. Then finally, she was able to get the strip started enough for her gloved fingers to grab it. She lifted his leg, thankful for the decreased gravity, and began to quickly wrap circles around the tear in his suit. She had no idea how bad his wound was but felt the pressure from the tape would help staunch the bleeding too. Once done, she tore off the strip and patted everything down firmly. She sat back on her knees and looked at his lifeless form. It appeared his suit was repressurized and the leak was sealed.

"Oh, Scott. Please be OK. Can you hear me?" she asked, taking his hand into hers. She couldn't feel a pulse or anything with her hands because of the bulky gloves.

What a selfish, chauvinistic . . . sweet, and gorgeous brute, she thought as she sat there. Tears began stinging her eyes. She knew he was emotionally struggling with their situation. What was his need to prove he was a big, strong man? Why do men even do that? Women don't want a macho pig, at least Mel didn't. Why didn't he just talk with her, let her try to comfort him. She was terrified too. They could have disabled this blasted gamma thing and then sat here together, looking into the most beautiful vista ever, knowing they'd saved the world. Holding each other. And now she was all alone awaiting her oxygen to deplete and just die.

Her pity party was just getting into full swing when it was interrupted by Scooter, now within range of her comms.

"Mel! Mel! If you can hear me, run!"

She looked back to see Scooter trying to run to her, but the low gravity had him bounding comically. He was waving his arms and legs to her to get up and move, run. She looked around for the threat and couldn't see anything but moon dust. Then in the distance, slowly rising out of a nearby canyon, was a black spacecraft that defined the word menacing. She froze in place. She couldn't leave Scott.

Chapter Twenty-One

Rodnell Cook steered the Viper into the canyon that led to the gamma-ray device. In his mind, he was battling with the decision of which side of the circumstances he wanted to commit to. One side argued to destroy the gamma-ray device for the greater good of humanity. He knew any future of continuing his pursuit of space development depended on that. However, even if he saved humanity, how would they view him after they learned he was party to its attempted destruction? Would they, from a scientific or engineering perspective, say what he had achieved was amazing enough to forgive him? Does society today forgive anyone anymore? Especially being a black man? He hated to think race would even be a factor, but like during any great catastrophe when people pull together for each other as fellow human beings, afterward things start to normalize and they eventually slip back into their comfort zones of bias and prejudice. He hated playing the race card, but dammit, there is some truth to it. Maybe Dr. Kerr was right all along. Maybe mankind had lost its way. Killing Mother Earth, he wasn't too concerned about. But maybe there was a bigger way that was being lost by the populous today . . . Compassion.

At this point he was reconsidering getting cold feet. People were digressing into narcissistic selfishness. So why fight the changing tide? He deserved everything he had worked for, and he wasn't about to surrender it to a bunch of narrow-minded hypocrites who would just steal what he had worked so hard to understand and create. He would side with Dr. Kerr. He would put his hurt feelings aside and suck it up. So there was no need to continue the gamma-ray device. He consulted his topographical map to see what vector would be best to reroute back to Earth from where he was.

****

Masters surveyed his surroundings. He had been in more than a few near-death experiences to keep his head level. Death, he didn't fear. But he would prefer to meet his maker on his own terms. If it came to it, he would eat his own gun. From where he stood, it looked like that may be his best course of action. It appeared the beasts had learned to hunt in packs. He could see them circling him strategically. The larger dogs in the shadows appeared to be the decision-makers. These gnashing at him were the pawns. He couldn't think of any way to get out of this that would end in nothing short of death.

He had seven rounds left in his magazine after firing one through that manipulative lush, Dr. Nizah's, deserving balls. Masters was a dead shot, he knew that. One bullet per beast would be great in thinning the herd to give him a fighting chance, but he knew as powerful as they were, it would take more than one bullet each. Maybe not even two. And they were fast, twice as fast as any normal dog of their respective breed. His car was about fifty yards away. Masters wasn't built for sprinting that span of ground quick enough. He slowly raised his arms up, ready to shoot the first dog that moved toward him. With arms extended he began to slowly walk backward, one slow step at a time.

A loud clang rang out in the distance. Each beast turned in unison to see what had caused it. Clang! Clang! Clang! To his left an Asian man in an apron stood outside a rear entry of what looked to be a kitchen. So the facility wasn't deserted after all. He began shouting at Masters.

"Run! Run!" Clang, clang, clang! He was beating two pots together, diverting the beasts' attention for just long enough for Masters to turn heel and sprint toward his car. Half the pack ran toward the cook clanging the pots; the other half began barking and took pursuit of Masters. He could hear their claws gripping at the concrete. He thought he might make it just as one of the huge dog beasts came from around the rear of his car. He raised his Glock and quickly squeezed two rounds into its head and chest. The beast bucked and twirled in the air, then recovered and ran toward him. Behind him, he could feel the pack closing in. He couldn't slow down. He raised his gun again and emptied his magazine into the charging beast as they closed in on each other. Several rounds missed, but a few hit home. The last one through the neck caused it to fall and tumble, skidding toward him. He leaped over it like an Olympic hurdler as it skidded underneath him. He landed in stride and kept running. Once at his car, he grabbed the handle and jumped in just as the pack descended on him, leaping onto the hood and gnashing at his door. Thankfully they couldn't get a purchase on anything they were biting at. Their huge tongues and jowls pressed against the slobbery windows, revealing rows of needle-sharp teeth.

Masters fished out a fresh magazine from the bag next to him and slammed it into place. As he racked the slide of his Glock, he pondered his next move. He couldn't shoot through the windshield, as it would weaken it enough for them to come through it. There were just too many to shoot his way out. Suddenly the car lurched and settled at an odd angle. A loud hiss of air could be heard. Another lurch and another loud hissing noise. They were taking out his tires.

There was a pause in all the vicious barking. The attacking dogs backed off, whimpering and yelping. The front of the car began to squat low. Masters could hear the suspension straining under the weight of something heavy stepping up onto the hood as it began to crinkle and cave. Now standing there was the most terrifying creature Masters had ever seen in his life. It was a dog, but the breed was lost on him. Maybe a bull mastiff if he had to wager a guess. It lowered its head, peering into the window at Masters with huge yellow eyes that seemed backlit, almost glowing. He could see the flexing of the huge muscles of the beast's shoulders, neck, and jaws. It started sniffing Masters through the glass as if to confirm what it was seeing. Then its muzzle pulled back into a wicked sneer, revealing huge rows of fangs. Streams of slimy drool drizzled down the window. Barely audible, the beast let out a growl so deep, Masters could feel it in his chest. Slowly, the beast put its huge paw on the windshield. Masters could see its thick pads squishing as it started to apply pressure. He could hear the glass straining like thin ice when stepped upon. A crack shot across his vision at a ragged angle. Then two more as a spiderweb appeared under the paw. Masters had little time to think before the beast pushed through all the way. He did the only thing he could think to do. The violent and excruciating death he was facing left him no choice. He placed the muzzle of his .45-caliber Glock in his mouth and hooked his thumb around the trigger.

****

Cook entered the coordinates for the Planet's Keepers base on Isla de los Estados into the navigation system. He then recognized the turn of the canyon ahead. Just beyond that was the gamma-ray device's location. He had come this far; he might as well give it a quick once-over before turning toward Earth. As he made the turn, he slowed and hovered up over the canyon's rim. There was the device, seemingly fine, but something was off. He slipped over the canyon edge and eased toward the device. In the distance, he thought he could make out a spacecraft that seemed to be sitting askew. He quickly engaged the weapons console and readied the minigun. *Where are the people? Maybe they are still in the craft.* He hovered closer to the gamma-ray device, careful to keep clear of its radiation plates. He saw various items scattered behind it and a tool tote. Still no sign of any people. Clear to him now was evidence the device had been tampered with.

He noticed a trail in the surface dust leading to a grouping of boulders. It looked like something, or someone, had been dragged by two people. There were footprints on each side of it. Someone was injured he surmised. He weighed his options. He could destroy the spacecraft with the minigun. That would doom them to their death, although the way it was leaning heavily to one side, it looked disabled already. Unless they were a threat, he couldn't kill in cold blood like that. *Are they a threat?* It was apparent they were trying to disable the gamma-ray device, which would thwart Dr. Kerr's plan. So much time and money had been put into the success of this project. Wasn't that threat enough? Maybe. He was certain Dr. Kerr would think so, but he wasn't Dr. Kerr. He wanted to think he was more human than that. So he wanted to find the people and see what was going on here. They could be dead already, for all he knew. There was no way to know how long they'd been here. He needed to inspect the gamma-ray device and repair any damage they may have done. He started the landing sequence. Once the Viper was on the surface, he slipped into a space suit.

"What do you see?" Mel asked Scooter. They had grabbed Scott and pulled him behind some large boulders. It wasn't much cover, but they didn't know what else to do.

"Looks like the ship is landing."

"We don't have any weapons, and anything hand-to-hand is useless in these suits," Mel fretted.

"Its hatch has opened. Someone is exiting that craft," Scooter said. He waited and watched, trying to come up with a plan. Cook walked down the gangplank holding a tool bag of his own and went to inspect the device.

"Damn," he said as he approached. One of the main power cables was cut. However, when he was here last and made the pulsing modification, he added a second capacitor board and another power cable connection for failover redundancy and load balancing. With only one cable still connected, the device was still operational, although the pulses might have been taking a couple minutes longer with fewer capacitor resources. However, the device should still have been effective in keeping the mutations recurring in the animals.

His eyes drifted to the spot where the tracks and the drag trail came together. He could see the tracks coming from the disabled spacecraft and several behind the gamma-ray device. Then a few feet back, there was a larger indention in the surface dust. Then the footprints appeared on either side of it and dragged whatever was

314

lying on the ground over behind those boulders in the distance. From all of this, he deduced someone had tried to cut the power cords without unplugging the capacitor boards in the access panel. That probably gave them a shock, maybe even killed them. Then when the Viper crested the canyon wall, they panicked, grabbed the person on the ground, and dragged him away.

So there were at least three of them. He wasn't sure if there might have been others still on the ship. On a ship that size, he doubted it. Now, being closer to it, he could see it was Russian. He knew Russians carried a small-caliber gun in their survival packs that also folded into a shovel and other tools. It was like a Swiss Army knife with a gun barrel. Nonetheless, it would be more than enough to kill him if used. He lowered his tool bag to the ground, then reached inside and pulled out a more formable weapon, a Desert Eagle. On Earth this thing was almost too big and heavy to be practical, but up here it was light as a feather and easy to grip and finger the trigger with a gloved hand. He stood and jacked a round into the gun's chamber and then followed the trail to the boulders.

"Aww hell . . . He's coming this way and packing a helluva pea shooter," Scooter said, ducking back down beside Mel.

"Oh, Scooter, I am so scared."

"Just breathe. Death comes for us all, even way the hell out here." He then had an idea. He looked at his wrist and punched the Scan button on his comm control. The digital frequency numbers started to roll. He knew which channel he and Mel were using. If the scanner stopped on another one, it should be that of the person coming toward him. If so, then maybe he could talk to him. This could all be a misunderstanding and the person wasn't a threat. He didn't think his comm was going to detect any new frequencies when it stopped. On his display was a different channel frequency than he and Mel were using. He took a breath and then spoke.

"Howdy there, partner." Silence ensued. Then someone spoke.

"Howdy, partner? That doesn't sound very Russian," Cook replied. He stopped walking and raised his gun.

"I hope not. But they do distill a pretty nice vodka."

"American. From Texas, I assume?"

"Yep, born and raised," Scooter replied, trying to keep his voice normal. He was as nervous as a long-tailed cat in a room full of rocking chairs.

"What's your business here, cowboy?"

"Welp, I usually wouldn't leave the great state of Texas, but with the stress of all those animals killing everybody, I needed a place to relax. Thought this was the perfect place. Didn't think I would meet anyone else up here though."

Mel saw the frequency they were talking on and switched over to listen.

"Are you armed?" Cook asked.

"What kinda cowpoke would I be if I wasn't packing iron? And a fair warning, I'm the fastest shot in these parts," Scooter bluffed, and Cook called him on it.

"You have three seconds to stand up and toss your invisible six-shooter away, or I will unload this hand cannon into those rocks. I think you'll learn, as I have, that bullets pack a much bigger punch up here, and I doubt those rocks will give you enough cover to protect you. Even a slight puncture in your suit will suit my needs. So what will it be?"

No one moved. Then rocks exploded above their heads as Cook fired a silent shot. Mel screamed and ducked. Both she and Scooter were peppered with debris, but no holes in their suits, yet. A huge chunk of rock was missing where the bullet had struck. Cook knew if he emptied his magazine, it would pulverize the remaining rocks and kill them. But he wasn't sure if he could do that. Especially if they were unarmed.

"Wait! Stop shooting! I'm standing up," Mel yelled, and stood. Scooter tried to grab her arm, but she pulled it away.

"Please don't shoot me," Mel begged, and stepped around the rocks. Cook was shocked to hear the voice of a female.

"Who are you people?" he asked.

"I'm Mel Florchett. Who we are is a long story, but our business here is to try to put an end to the vicious killing on Earth by disabling that device over there. We spent two days in a crash course on how to travel here and do it. Our ship crashed, and we're stuck. So if you are going to shoot me, do it now. I'm dead in a couple hours anyways."

Cook stood there still aiming his gun. He could hear the desperation in the girl's voice. It was obvious they were not properly trained for this, yet here they were, and they had come very close to succeeding. This took guts and bravery he didn't think he even had. He respected that. These people were heroes trying to save humanity. Was he really a villain in the name of a utopian idea? No, these people needed help, and he wanted to help them. He wanted to help humanity. Mother Earth would have to find another way to survive.

"Well, you failed," Cook replied.

"I know. And someone I care for very much has paid dearly." She looked back toward the rocks that Scott lay behind, not knowing if he even was alive. Scooter joined her and took her hand. Cook was moved by their courage.

"But we will succeed together," Cook said, and lowered his gun. He walked to them and offered his hand.

"I'm Rodnell Cook. Pleasure to meet you, Mel." They shook and then he turned to Scooter and they shook.

"Just call me Scooter. And that guy back there sunnin' his belly is Scott."

"Let's get him loaded onto my ship where we can take a look at him," Cook said, and made his way over to Scott. He handed Mel the Desert Eagle. He and Scooter were able to pick Scott up easily and load him into the Viper. Cook shut the hatch and released the air lock. They entered the main cabin and laid Scott on the floor. Quickly, they all stripped out of their space suits and took off Scott's helmet. Mel could now check his pulse.

"Oh, thank God! It's there but it's weak," she said excitedly. She stroked his cheek. He was very pale.

"Let's pack snacks and make some tracks, Rodnell. This guy needs a meat wagon ASAP," Scooter said, then gestured toward the copilot seat next to Cook.

"I'd be honored, friend." Cook nodded, and Scooter slid in and fastened his harness. The Viper lifted up and took flight, making a wide arc and then turning back toward the moon.

"Uhm, I know this is a vast universe up here, but I am pretty sure Earth is attaway." Scooter pointed back over his shoulder.

"What? And not finish what we all came here to do?" Cook said with a crooked smile. At that moment a rocket sped forth into view, leaving a cylindrical trail of smoke. The missile struck the gamma-ray device squarely, obliviating it completely.

"Hell yeah!" Scooter exclaimed. Mel had joined them with an arm around both their necks and squeezed them tightly together, then kissed them both on their cheek.

"I love you guys!" she gushed.

"Hey, do I get any of that?" a voice asked behind her.

"Scott!" She whirled around to see him sitting up. She jumped on him, knocking him back, straddling him in a full guard, pinning his arms over his head.

"You give?" she asked him, their noses almost touching.

"For you? Everything I have. Always," Scott whispered back. Mel dipped her lips and kissed him deeply, and he returned the effort.

Scooter and Cook stared at the couple's embrace for a moment, and then Scooter turned to Cook and asked, "So what other goodies you got in this thing?"

"Check this out," Cook replied as both men turned their attention forward and started geeking out over the Viper's other cool features, leaving Scott and Mel to their business.

Cook made sure he was far enough away when he launched the missile this time. He turned the Viper around and zoomed toward Earth in deep conversation with Scooter about all things aerospace.

****

Masters could taste the tang of the gun oil and spent powder residue from the barrel on his tongue. The beast had inverted the windshield into thousands of pieces, the clear safety laminate punctured by its claws. It would be on him in just seconds now. Masters wrapped his lips tight, squeezed his eyes, and slowly applied pressure to the trigger. He felt it start to squeeze and waited for the buck of the recoil. Then that would be that. Then he wouldn't care if he was to be a chew toy for these abominable muts.

A couple more pounds of pressure, Masters thought as the pull of the trigger furthered. Then the front of the car bounced up and down, landing normally on flat tires. The beast had jumped off. He quickly opened his eyes and removed the pistol. He didn't realize he had been holding his breath and breathed heavily, looking around to see what happened. All the growling and barking had ceased. He only heard a few whimpers and yelps in the distance. He couldn't see out and decided to crack his door for a peek. He could tell the beasts had left.

He slowly stood up from his seat and looked around. Dawn had set in, casting an eerie light across the concrete campus. Shadows lay about everywhere in the distance. It took him a second to see they were the beasts, or the hulls of them. His gun still in hand, he exited the car. Pointing it at the nearest shadow, he crept over to it slowly. It was a Doberman pinscher. It was clearly dead, stuck in a halfway mutated and halfway normal state. He looked around. All of the dogs lay dead in a similar state. He looked up at the still-visible moon and thought he saw a twinkle of light. He knew then the team had succeeded in destroying the gamma-ray device. He smiled big and pumped a celebratory fist into the air. Humanity was saved.

Chapter Twenty-Two

Dr. Kerr awoke in his office. He often slept on his couch when he had an early morning ahead. His excitement for today had kept him awake, so he had taken a powerful sleeping pill. He had to get some sleep. Today was too important to be groggy. His cell was slammed with texts, emails, and missed calls as usual. He would check them at breakfast. He showered and dressed, then walked to the engineering lab to see about this morning's business before heading to eat. It was empty. Puzzled, he headed to the launch area. Everyone was probably there readying the first pod for launch. He found that he didn't need Cook for this. Turns out, the crew was well versed in the launching sequence and showed him the steps during several test runs the prior day. It really wasn't all that difficult. The technology was so well automated a bright twelve-year-old could pull off a successful launch. He pressed his thumb to the biometric scanner. The doors slid open. This area was empty, too, silent. He made an announcement yesterday evening for the first group to ready their belongings and meet at the launching area at dawn. They should have been filing in by now. What was holding them up? And where had the launch crew gotten off to? This was not the day to sleep in. Rage filled his gut as he marched to the elevators. It seemed the entire underwater portion of the complex was empty. He punched the button for the surface.

While riding the elevator up, he decided to check his phone. His news app was swollen with breaking news alerts. He began reading them. He couldn't believe what he was seeing. *This can't be.* The elevator opened to a hallway. He turned left toward the wing of the housing units. All empty. He walked by the cafeteria and saw an LCD TV was turned to the news. He walked to it and unmuted the volume:

"If you're just tuning in this morning, it seems that the animal apocalypse is over. Early this morning, reports from all over the world were being broadcast of mutated animals lying down and dying. It seems whatever was causing the evolutions in these killing machines has stopped. Mankind is breathing a sigh of relief, but is left with the burden of hundreds of millions of human deaths and animal carcasses to deal with. People are beginning to leave their shelters and put the pieces of their lives back together, searching for surviving friends and loved ones or, worse, those that didn't. Law enforcement is working to restore order and safety. Lawmakers in Washington, DC, have called for an emergency session to discuss how best to start getting the country back to normal. This was a dark period for our entire world, but like so many dark times before, mankind persevered and will survive to see another day. I'm Tiffany Cross reporting maybe the biggest triumph ever for the human race. Back to you in the studio, Eddie."

"Arrrggh!" Dr. Kerr shouted as he flung the remote at the TV, shattering the plastic screen. "This can't be! I'm gonna kill Cook," he seethed as he stomped back to the elevator and slammed the button to go back down to his office. Cook had surely gone rogue and would tell all about this conspiracy. Dr. Kerr knew he soon would be a hunted man. He needed to escape before the island was raided. Fortunately, he had packed his travel luggage already. He grabbed it and headed for the launching area. Yesterday during the test runs, an engineer was doing everything from a tablet. He began searching for it. He found it in a charging station in the control room.

"Yes," he said to himself, and snatched off its cradle. He then headed to the first travel pod and entered. It was already attached to the catapult. He strapped in the front seat, powered on the tablet, and began preparing the launch sequences. Another twenty minutes and the earth could kiss his ass. He would be heading to the moon colony. And the first order of business was to see if the gamma-ray device could be brought back online. *We'll see how mankind survives a second-wave apocalypse.* And he would deal with Cook later.

****

"The weapon system is online and ready to fire. We're awaiting your order, Mr. President," Air Force General Malin Thomas said from a conference phone. A small group of the highest-ranking military and government officials was gathered around a large table in the Oval Office. Seated along the far wall were Dr. Sheltie and Rob. They all turned to look at a huge LCD screen on the wall. On the screen, from a NASA secret satellite, was a zoomed-in view of the Isla de los Estados islands off the southernmost coast of South America.

"Director Lett, have all the inhabitants been evacuated and detained?" the president asked Trey Lett.

"Yes, sir. The last transport plane left over an hour ago. They should be well enough away by now with all passengers accounted for," announced Lett. Just then the door opened and Benjamin Masters entered the room. His flight back to DC recently landed, and he was flown to the White House via a navy chopper. He could see everyone focused on the screen. He took a seat next to Rob. Dr. Sheltie reached over and squeezed his hand, and all three leaned together.

"Have I missed anything?" Masters whispered.

"Nothing yet, really," Rob answered him.

"Alek, are the Russians tuned into the sat feed? Can you all see the view from our satellite?" the president asked.

"We see it crystal clear," Aleksandr Antonov responded in accented English from the conference phone. "And the guests of honor just arrived, you may be happy to know," Alek added.

"Let's get this here dog an' pony show on the road. Imma whooped puppy. Any of youins got any of that good vodka?" Scooter's Texas drawl could be heard in the background. Dr. Sheltie laughed and gave Rob a comforting squeeze and kissed him on his head, knowing that Mel was back on Earth safe and sound.

The president turned and surveyed the room. "Ladies and gentlemen, I realize I should make a statement for posterity. But I just really want to convey my deepest sympathies and condolences for all who lost loved ones in this senseless, single worst act of terrorism this world has ever seen." He paused and looked at each person. Then he slammed his fist on the table. "Now let's get this son of a bitch."

The room erupted in cheers.

"General Thomas, fire at will," the president ordered.

"On my mark in three . . . two . . . one . . . fire," the general said matter-of-factly.

****

Eight thousand miles into space, a top secret weapon was orbiting Earth waiting to be initialized. It wasn't nuclear, because nuclear weapons in space were prohibited under the Outer Space Treaty signed by 109 different countries in 1967. However, its impact on the earth's surface would deliver the same punch, but with no nuclear fallout. It had never been used, until now.

The Rods of God it was called. This hypersonic weapon was one of the most simple, yet one of the most powerful weapons the United States had ever created, with the explosive power of an intercontinental ballistic missile. It was composed of a bundle of telephone-pole-sized tungsten rods, twenty feet long, one foot in diameter, and dropped from orbit, reaching a speed of up to ten times the speed of sound. During the Vietnam War, the US discovered that dropping what they called "Lazy Dog" bombs at three hundred feet, reaching a velocity of 500 mph, was a very effective weapon. These were simply solid steel pieces, less than two inches long, fitted with fins. There was no explosive—they were simply dropped by the hundreds from planes flying above Vietnam. They called this kinetic bombardment, Project Thor, which in time gave birth to the Rods of God.

Dr. Kerr finished the last keying of the launch sequence. Not that it was necessary, but he felt like he wanted to countdown his launch.

"Launching in twenty seconds . . . ten seconds . . . five . . . four . . . three . . . two . . . one, ignition," he said to himself. The catapult engaged, causing the g-forces to pin him hard into his seat. He heard the brief woosh of the one hundred feet of water before he was slung into the air. For a moment he felt weightless as the inertia from the catapult fizzled out, just before the rockets engaged. The sky was a beautiful blue. In his peripheral vision he thought he saw a glimmer of light in the blue sky. Then he thought he could hear the sound barrier being broken. It would be the last thing he saw and heard as his life was snuffed out in an instant. The only thing left of him and his transport craft was a mist of pink wafting in the air as one of the tungsten rods skewered the transport craft and in it, Dr. Kerr.

The bulk of tungsten poles hit slightly off the coast of the islands, vaporizing the ocean water as it impacted the underground lair of the Planet's Keepers. A bubble of scorched seawater rose into the air hundreds of feet and over three hundred yards wide. Then a huge plume erupted, sending debris in every direction. All of this happening in just hundredths of a second. The underground facility was decimated. A huge tidal wave was created from the impact and slammed hard onto the islands, destroying everything on them but leaving the islands themselves intact. The buildings and all infrastructure were wiped out and now floated out to sea in shattered chunks. The whole scene was of devastation. A cleansing. The Planet's Keepers were destroyed in an instant.

In Moscow, Russia, the room erupted in celebration. Scooter toasted Nakita, throwing back a shot of vodka, and then they embraced. Nakita breathed in deeply and held Scooter with all her strength. He returned the embrace, and then they stared into each other's eyes and began to kiss. Scott sat in a wheelchair. Mel draped herself around him from behind, cheek to cheek. Neither ever thought they would have made it back to Earth alive. Yet here they were, and the emotions from all the stress leading to this point left salty streaks down their cheeks.

****

Back in the Oval Office, champagne was being uncorked and poured into glass flutes being passed around. The president cheered as he tossed back his champagne. Dr. Sheltie embraced Rob with so much force he thought she might crush him. Masters walked over and joined the group hug, and then they pulled apart.

"Master Rob. Thank you for being patient with me. I know I haven't been the friendliest since our first meeting back in Dallas. But I want to express my appreciation to you," Masters said.

"Don't worry about it. It's all in the past," Rob replied, smiling.

****

Rodnell Cook sat in his chair in the conference room in Moscow, Russia, still staring at the huge LCD screen. All that was left of the view was floating evidence of the destruction. Yes, he was grateful he was alive. Yes, he felt in his heart he had chosen right by rescuing Scooter, Scott, and Mel and then destroying the gamma-ray device. Yes, he felt satisfaction knowing Dr. Kerr received justice. But he still couldn't help but feel a bit sad. The debris and destruction floating in the sea water was all that was left of his life's work now. His team was detained somewhere and awaiting a trial. Hell, he would probably be indicted himself. With this in mind, he stood slowly and silently slipped out of the room. He knew he was on the right side of history, but would it be seen that way in the immediate future? He didn't know, but he knew he needed to get somewhere safe to think about everything just in case. The cold wind whipped across him as he walked out onto the curb and hailed a passing cab. He entered the back seat and instructed the driver, then sat back and watched Moscow's city center disappear into the distance.

Epilogue

6 Weeks Later

Rob and Mel Florchett sat at a patio table at a pizza joint called We the Pizza, overlooking the National Mall in Washington, DC. Mel lay back in her chair letting the sun soak into her long, lean limbs.

"I'll never get enough sunshine. Russia is too damn cold, and the moon is too damn stressful. Give me a sunny day here on Earth in the USA any day," Mel said, her eyes closed, allowing the sun's warmth to penetrate her skin. Rob sat in the shade of the table's umbrella, just fine.

"Are you ready to head back to Dallas?" Rob asked.

"Not really. I have nowhere to go."

"Have you given any thought to going to college? We could get an apartment."

"I don't know. I want to be with Scott, and we haven't decided how that might work. I am just enjoying every breath I take right now. Not worried about anything else."

Rob understood that. Not so long ago he had been in a situation that made him not want life to go on. But now, being here with his sister, he savored every minute of it.

"What do you think Dr. Sheltie wants to talk to us about today?" Mel wondered.

"Who knows? I know her and Masters have gotten super close the last few weeks. Probably an engagement announcement."

"Yeah, I could see that. Good for them. They make a cute couple." Mel laughed.

"Are you ready to be center stage tomorrow in front of the whole world?"

"Not really. I am honored to be recognized for saving humanity, but I don't think I am ready for all the fame that will come from it," Mel said thoughtfully. Tomorrow the president scheduled an awards ceremony for Mel, Scott, Scooter, and Masters for their role in saving the world. He was making as much political hay as he could. What better way to celebrate the bravery of Americans than to plaster himself in front of all the media coverage? His second term was coming to a fast close, so he was thinking about what next afterward. No doubt he would love the cush job of traveling the global speaker circuit raking in all sorts of cash talking about his part in everything.

"There they are," Rob said, seeing Masters and Dr. Sheltie making their way onto the back patio of the pizzeria. They were holding hands when Dr. Sheltie spotted the two siblings and rushed over. Rob and Mel hadn't seen them for a few days. Masters was very busy debriefing the powers that be on his role in stopping Dr. Nizah from detonating that dirty bomb and taking out most of the US electrical grid. Mel stood and embraced Dr. Sheltie.

"Master Rob. Good to see you. And Mel," Masters said, his arm extended to shake hands. They all took seats as the waiter came around to take their food-and-drink orders. Once that was settled, Masters's demeanor took a serious tone.

"I wanted us to get together one last time before the ceremony tomorrow. It's going to change all of our lives forever." He paused, clearly struggling with what he wanted to say next. Rob sensed this and swallowed hard. Mel's emerald eyes moved from Masters to Dr. Sheltie, whose gaze was turned down to the napkin she was folding and unfolding nervously.

"So Dr. Sheltie has something she wants to tell you," Masters finally said.

"Well, it's something I've wanted to tell you both since we all met several weeks ago," Dr. Sheltie said. She paused, struggling.

"What is it?" Rob prompted. Dr. Sheltie sighed heavily. After a long pause to gather her composure she whispered, "Nancy Florchett is not your biological mother. I am," now looking them both in the eyes. She dared not say anything else until the kids had a chance to absorb that bit of knowledge. Rob and Mel exchanged looks, both dumbstruck at this revelation.

"I don't understand," Rob said in shock. Dr. Sheltie turned to Masters, clearly wanting him to explain the situation now that the cat was out of the bag.

"Julie Sanderson is Nancy Florchett's real name. She is a special agent with the CIA like me. To ensure the secrets from the 1970's Supermoon incident were never revealed by your father, whom they knew had psychological issues that could become a risk, the CIA introduced her to him. Her job was to assume the role of a single socialite within the community. Your father was immediately smitten with her, and after just a month of dating, he unexpectedly proposed to her." Masters paused. Both Mel's and Rob's mouths hung open. He continued, "The agency decided this would work perfectly, but Julie had her doubts and didn't want to go through with it. However, the agency always wins, and so they got married. The first several months were OK. Julie, or Nancy as she was known, fit in quite well and found your dad to be quite charming and affable. So this arrangement was tolerable. But then your father started pushing to have children. The Agency tried to push Julie into getting pregnant, but she said absolutely not. This was going too far and she put her foot down. To delay your dad's wishes, they needed a reason why Nancy Florchett wouldn't want to have children. That would certainly cause a problem in their relationship, so she claimed she may have some sort of disorder that would prohibit a pregnancy. Their doctor, Dr. Klaskin, whom Dr. Sheltie was performing her clinicals with and was on our payroll, went on with the ruse, claiming Nancy was barren and couldn't have children. The idea of a surrogate mother was floated and your father agreed to it. So he went to a fertility clinic to collect his sperm. Meanwhile Dr. Sheltie was approached by Dr. Klaskin about carrying the child, and she agreed. She then was inseminated, and nine months later Master Rob was born." Masters paused as the pizza was being lowered onto the table. Once the waiter was out of earshot, he continued.

"That first year with Master Rob was very good. Your father began pushing for another child in hopes of it being a girl. Again Julie was adamantly opposed, now becoming agitated about the whole scheme. She began creating issues in her relationship with your dad, drinking heavily and other erratic behavior. Your father's mental balance began to unravel with how Nancy was acting. He started to become paranoid and accused her of cheating on him. The agency didn't like the way things were turning between the two of them and approached Dr. Sheltie about being the surrogate to another child. She agreed. The next nine months wore Julie down, and she was threatening to ditch the whole project. The agency couldn't allow this, and a tension began to form between the two. Your father, now caught in the middle of it, had his first mental breakdown. He was institutionalized for a month before Mel was born."

"So Mel and I are truly brother and sister though, right?" Rob asked, anger forming in his gut from the news he was hearing.

"Yes! Yes, of course you are," Dr. Sheltie answered emphatically. Mel sat there silent trying to absorb everything. She couldn't remember much about Nancy Florchett, so this news was only shocking because it was new to her, but she wasn't taking it as hard as Rob, it seemed. His cheeks had reddened deeply as he thought through the details.

"I loved my mom," Rob said quietly. He put his head in his hands. Mel reached over and rubbed his back for support.

"So keep going," Mel directed, becoming angry herself, but only because Rob was reeling.

"So I was inserted into the situation. Julie was becoming unstable and needed support, but what I gave her was strictly professional, nothing more," Masters explained.

"So you didn't have an affair with her?" Rob asked, looking up in disbelief.

"No, Master Rob, I didn't."

"But you led me to believe it was so?"

"It wasn't my choice. That was a conclusion you came to, and for me to explain the truth would mean revealing the whole stupid charade. I am so sorry for that," Masters said, his eyes becoming misty.

"So that's it? Mom had enough once Dad lost his sanity and was committed for good and dumped us on a neighbor and ran away?" Rob asked in disbelief.

"Pretty much. At that point Julie was alone with two young kids that weren't hers and no clear path out of the whole thing," Masters said.

"Unbelievable," Rob muttered. He looked at Dr. Sheltie and saw the remorse in her puffy eyes, now gushing streams of tears down her cheeks. His heart ached for her. Over the last couple months they had become very close, and looking back, he now understood her passion for saving Mel.

"And you truly didn't know who I was when I showed up in your office that day?" Rob asked Dr. Sheltie.

"No. Not until you told me your name. I couldn't believe it, but knew I had to help you. Then when you told me about Mel, I became obsessed with saving her and trying to reunite us all," she said as a sob caught in her throat.

"At least we know the truth now," Mel said quietly. All four of them sat there in silence. The pizza had now long been cold. Nobody had an appetite at this point.

"There is one more thing," Dr. Sheltie said, sucking in a breath.

"Oh no." Rob sighed, preparing for the worst.

"Um, well. You... you both have a sister," Dr. Sheltie choked out.

"A . . . sister?" Mel asked, now very surprised.

"Yes. Mel . . ." Dr. Sheltie paused to breathe, then said, "You have a twin."

Mel's breath caught in her throat. A twin. A copy of herself? How could this be?

"With the second pregnancy, I had twin girls. Her name is Michelle. She doesn't know about any of this either. I felt you both should know first. I am planning on telling her tonight." Dr. Sheltie was crying full force now.

Masters wrapped his long arm around her, and she began sobbing into his shoulder. Rob and Mel sat there stunned.

****

The stage was set in the Rose Garden, off the Oval Office of the White House. Chairs were in place to accommodate two hundred people, with even more media. Every news channel in the free world was there to see the president present the four with honorary medals. Mel sat on the stage next to Scott, who held her hand. Beside him was Scooter and Masters. The president was giving a speech about the tenacity of each of them, braving the unknown to save the world from the destruction of the radical environmentalist group, the Planet's Keepers. It was obvious in the news over the last several weeks since the incident that all the elite support of the Planet's Keepers had waned very quickly. Those who were staunch supporters were now staunch critics. No one wanted to be associated with the group any longer. They were toxic.

All of those collected from the headquarters in South America were being detained and questioned, and several federal courts were determining if their involvement qualified as treason. These hearings would go on for months to come, as each rich-and-powerful person had created several dream teams of lawyers. This made the OJ Simpson trial miniscule in scope and size.

The president wrapped up his speech and asked Masters and Scott to join him at the podium. He introduced Masters and explained his contribution in stopping what could have been the worst terrorist attack on US soil since 9/11. The president then awarded Masters the Trailblazer Award. It was the CIA's equivalent to the military's Medal of Honor. They shook hands and posed for the cameras. Next, Scott was introduced as the president gushed over his bravery in the lunar expedition to destroy the gamma-ray device. He, too, was awarded the Trailblazer Award. Next was Scooter. The president became very animated describing the heroics of this pilot, how he'd saved Diego's life from the demon dogs and then rescued an entire Mexican village from the apocalyptic cattle nightmare. He then went on to pilot a spacecraft to the moon with only two days of training. Scooter stood there in his cowboy hat and boots, surveying the crowd, chewing his gum and soaking up the glory.

Next it was Mel's turn. The president described her unmatched courage both in saving the Mexican village and destroying the gamma-ray device on the moon. She was halfway paying attention to the accolades being bestowed upon her. She heard the medal awarded to her was the highest civilian award, the Presidential Medal of Freedom.

"Mel? Are you OK?" Scott leaned over and asked.

"What? Yes . . . why?" There was a roar of applause. Then she realized the president was motioning her to the podium to receive her medal. It was all she could do to tear her eyes off of herself, sitting there in the front row between Dr. Sheltie and Rob. Identical in every way, Michelle Florchett sat there applauding Mel with her mom, her brother, and the rest of the world.

The End